POWER UP™

BOOM! BOX™

BOOM! BOX

A catalog record of this book is available from OCLC and from the BOOM! Studios website, www.boom-studios.com, on the Librarians page.

BOOM! Studios, 5670 Wilshire Boulevard, Suite 450, Los Angeles, CA 90036-5679. Printed in China. First Printing.

ISBN: 978-1-60886-837-7, eISBN: 978-1-61398-508-3

CREATED BY

KATE **LETH** & MATT **CUMMINGS**

WRITTEN BY
KATE **LETH**

ILLUSTRATED BY
MATT **CUMMINGS**

LETTERED BY
JIM **CAMPBELL**

COVER BY
MATT **CUMMINGS**

DESIGNER
MICHELLE **ANKLEY**

EDITOR
SHANNON **WATTERS**

CHAPTER ONE

WHEN THEY FIRST LOOKED UP AND BEGAN TO CHART THE SKIES, THEY PREDICTED:
"A STAR WILL DIE AS ANOTHER IS BORN, AND SO WILL THEY BE CHOSEN.
"FOUR WARRIORS TO CHAMPION US INTO A NEW AGE--A TIME OF PEACE.
"OF STRENGTH.
"OF CELEBRATION."
IN THE OLDEST LANGUAGE, BY THE WISEST HANDS, IT WAS WRITTEN.

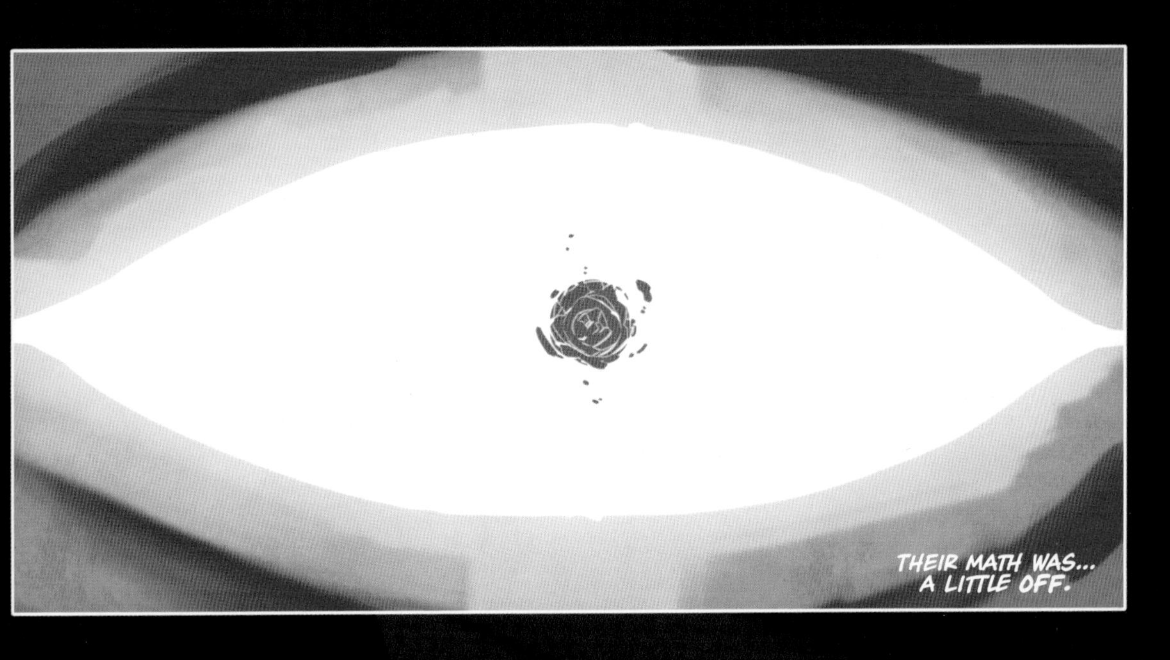
THEIR MATH WAS... A LITTLE OFF.

KNIFE PARTY...
I HATE VACATIONS
FRANKEN BURG!!
THIS SUMMER

FWAH?

OH NOOOOOOO. WHY? WHY? STOP THIS.

HI, KAREN.
AMIE! THANK GOODNESS YOU'RE AWAKE! IT'S AN EMERGENCY!

WHAT'S UP?

YOU DIDN'T CLOCK OUT YESTERDAY, AND SO I HAD TO GO BACK IN AND REBOOT THE COMPUTER SYSTEM!

IT TOOK SEVEN MINUTES AND HONESTLY, AMIE, THIS IS THE SECOND TIME THIS HAS HAPPENED!

--IF YOU SHIRK YOUR RESPONSIBILITIES, IT MAKES ME LOOK BAD AS AN EMPLOYER--
Murder.
SHE

--VERY DISAPPOINTED IN YOU, IT'S TIME YOU TOOK THINGS A LITTLE MORE SERIOUSLY--

--AND, FURTHERMORE, THIS OTHER THING I HAVE TO SAY IS--
MORNING, HOT STUFF.

--WANT THE BEST FOR YOU, I SEE ALL THIS POTENTIAL BUT YOU'RE JUST--
I GOT IT, BOSS. WON'T FORGET TO CLOCK OUT NEXT TIME. SEE YOU AT NOON.

:SIGH:
CLICK!

I'M VERY DISAPPOINTED IN YOUR JOB PERFORMANCE, ARDMORE. YOU'RE NOT REALLY SHOWING INITIATIVE.

IF YOU'VE GOT TIME TO LEAN, YOU'VE GOT TIME TO CLEAN, THAT'S WHAT I SAY!

DANGIT.

STAY.

SAL's

PJs, VERY NOW. I LIKE THIS LOOK, AMIE.
HERMIT CHIC. IT'S A THING.
YOU'RE LIVING THE LIFE, KID.
MILK
MILK

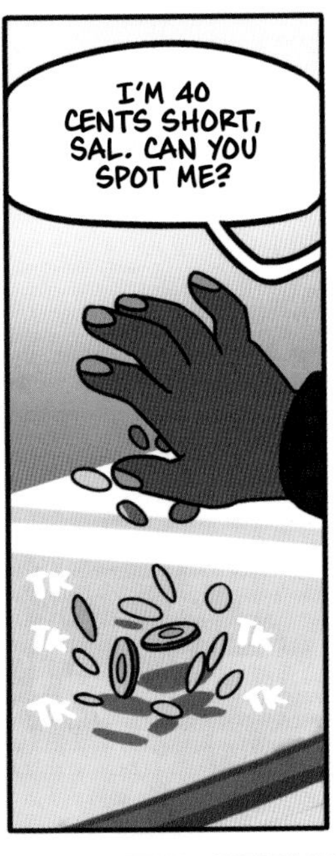
I'M 40 CENTS SHORT, SAL. CAN YOU SPOT ME?
TK
TK
TK
TK
TK

OF COURSE. DO WE LOOK LIKE--
NO. POUR SOME OUT. RIGHT NOW.

THANKS, GUYS! I THINK I'LL HAVE MORE HOURS NEXT WEEK!
GOOD LUCK!
WE KNOW WHERE YOU LIVE!

CAN I WEAR PYJAMAS?

VVVVVROOM

TING!
AMIE!

HI, KAREN.
YOU'RE THIRTEEN MINUTES LATE.
I KNOW. IT'S ALL THE CONSTRUCTION, MY BUS GOT HELD UP.
CAN YOU NOT TAKE ONE THAT LEAVES EARLIER?

IF I TAKE THAT ONE, I GET HERE 45 MINUTES BEFORE MY SHIFT.
IT CERTAINLY SEEMS BETTER THAN BEING LATE.

HOPEFULLY THE ROADS CLEAR UP.
IMAGINE IF WE HAD CUSTOMERS WAITING!

IMAGINE.
TUMBLE TUMBLE

TING!
HEY, YOU NEED SOME HELP WITH ALL THAT?
HA! NO, I WISH. THANKS. I'M GOOD.
CRICKETS?
SURE. HOW MANY?
OH, A DOZEN. LET'S GO CRAZY.
FOR YOU?
MY SON. HE DROPPED THE LAST BOX IN THE BATHROOM. IT'S BEEN A TIME.
YEEK, I'M SORRY. SUGAR AND BREADCRUMBS, IF THAT HELPS. THEY'RE ATTRACTED TO IT.
HUH. WELL, THANKS. HAVE A NICE DAY, WILL YOU?
RAT'S NEST
SURE THING.

GOT TO GO MOVE MY CAR. I'LL BE BACK IN FIFTEEN MINUTES.

CAN I TRUST YOU?
YES, I THINK I CAN HANDLE IT.

DING!
PLEASE TRY NOT TO BREAK ANYTHING.

I'M PRETTY SURE I CAN--

WHAT?

GASP

AH, GEEZ. NO, COME ON.

WH... SILAS! YOU'RE OKAY!

SPLOOP

DING!
DING
AAAH, WE'RE CLOSED JUST NOW!

OKAY, WHAT?

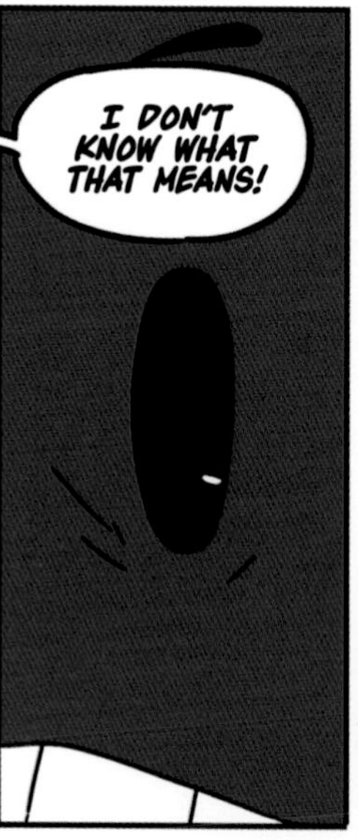
I DON'T KNOW WHAT THAT MEANS!

WHAT IS HAPPENING?!

SSSMASH
AAAH!

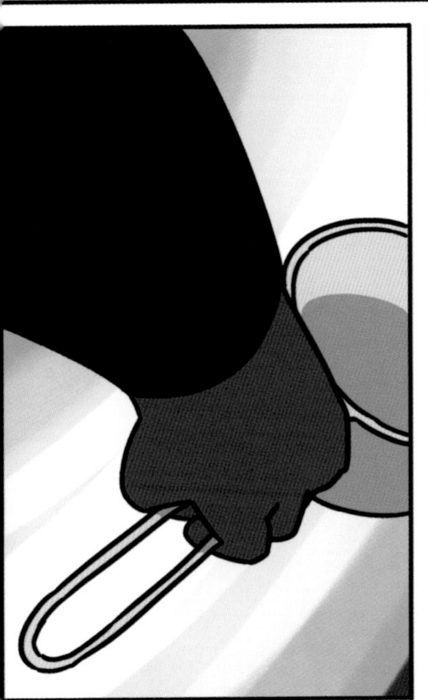

HAH!
KLANG

NOT... HAH.

SSSSSSS

!
NO!

SSSSSS
MY HANDS...

FOO——OM

KSHH!!

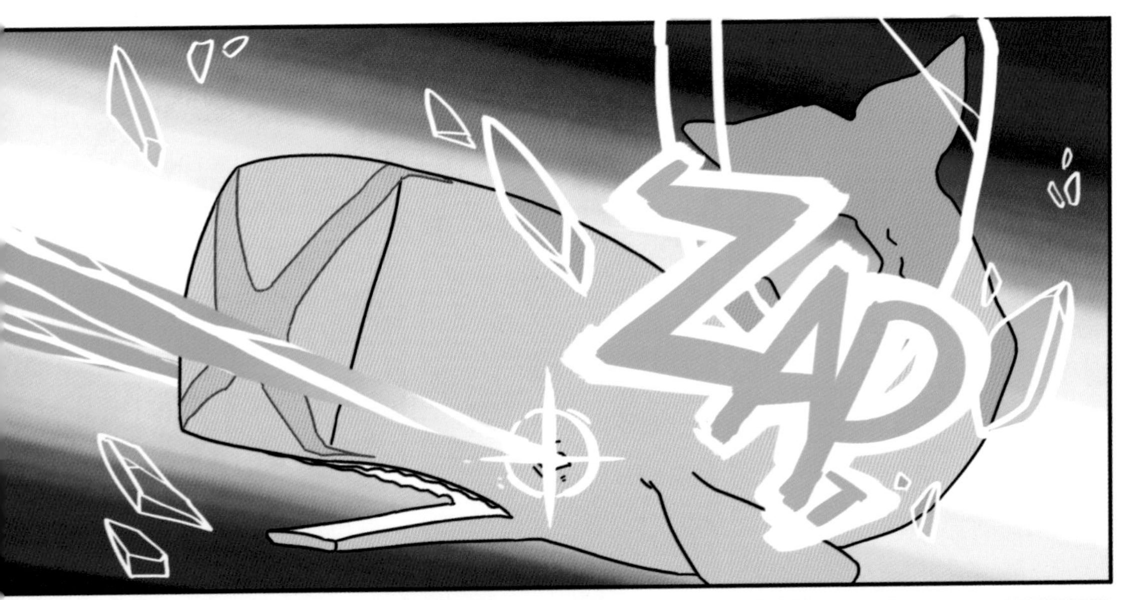
ZAP

?

VVVVV

POP!

SPLISH
SPLOOSH

TING!

MY STORE.

I--
WHAT HAPPENED? HOW? DID SOMEONE BREAK IN?

BUT--
WHAT DID HE LOOK LIKE? OR SHE? ARE THEY STILL HERE?!

NO! I MEAN, SOMETHING ATTACKED ME. DIDN'T YOU SEE THE LIGHT?

WAIT, DON'T TOUCH MY--!

HUH? IT DIDN'T SHOCK--
DID YOU STOP THEM? DID THEY--OH NO, DID THEY GET THE FLOAT?
IT DIDN'T TAKE ANYTHING.
KAREN, I'M SERIOUS, DID YOU SEE THAT HUGE EXPLOSION OF LIGHT? IT WAS EVERYWHERE.

OH, YOU'RE SAFE, YOU'RE SAFE.
THANK GOODNESS.

I'M CALLING THE COPS.
WAIT!

I CAN'T... WHATEVER WAS HERE, IT WASN'T HUMAN.
YOU MEAN, LIKE, AN ANIMAL?
KIND OF, BUT NOT REALLY. IT WAS WEARING A SUIT.

AMIE, ARE YOU OKAY? YOU'RE PROBABLY IN SHOCK.
I KNOW WHAT I SAW. I MEAN, I THINK I DO.

MAYBE... MAYBE YOU SHOULD HEAD HOME, BEFORE THE POLICE COME.
NO, I'M FINE. I JUST CAN'T FIGURE OUT WHAT HAPPENED. YOU'RE SURE YOU DIDN'T SEE ALL THAT LIGHT?

YOUR MIND MESSES WITH YOU IN STRESSFUL SITUATIONS. AMIE, I'M GLAD YOU'RE OKAY, BUT YOU CAN'T SAY THAT STUFF TO ANYONE. YOU KNOW HOW THAT SOUNDS?
I GUESS...

TING!

CHANNEL FOUR. GOT A MINUTE?

HEY! HON, LOOK, AMIE'S ON TV!
HUH? FOR WHAT?

– VOL +

POLICE ARE ADVISING RESIDENTS AND BUSINESSES OF THE AREA AROUND PRIMROSE STREET TO BE ON ALERT AFTER A VIOLENT INCIDENT AT LOCAL PET STORE *THE RATS' NEST.*
THE RATS' NEST

OWNER KAREN ESPINOSA SAYS NOTHING WAS TAKEN, BUT HER SOLE EMPLOYEE WAS ATTACKED.
I WAS OUT MOVING MY CAR AND WHEN I CAME BACK, IT HAD ALREADY HAPPENED.

I'M JUST SO GLAD SHE'S SAFE.

OH, AMIE!

AMIE BLOOM, 23, DESCRIBES THE ASSAILANT AS WEARING A DISGUISE AND SPEAKING AN UNIDENTIFIED FOREIGN LANGUAGE.
THAT'S NOT WHAT I SAID! DID NOBODY SEE THE LIGHT? THERE WAS THIS HUGE--

SHE'S IN SHOCK, THE POOR THING. MUST BE AWFUL. I WISH I HAD BEEN THERE TO STOP HIM!

I DON'T KNOW. MAYBE I WAS IMAGINING THINGS.

I SAW THIS LIGHT...
CAL's

IT WAS EVERYWHERE.
!

JUST FOR A SECOND, BEFORE THE ATTACK.
I FELT...
I FELT LIKE I COULD FLY.

CAN I SETTLE UP, CAL? JUST THE ONE.
SURE THING, KEVIN. YOU IN A RUSH?
HAVING A WEIRD DAY. THINK I NEED TO LIE DOWN.
SANDY, HON, DO WE HAVE ANY ROOT BEER?
HMMM? OH, I'LL CHECK.

SNAP

I DUNNO. I SUPPOSE THAT ALL SOUNDS PRETTY RIDICULOUS. NOBODY ELSE SAW IT.

GUESS IT'S JUST ME.

CHAPTER TWO

CAROLINE?
ARE YOU... ARE YOU THERE?
AIIIIIIIEEEEEE!

YOU'RE BACK, FROM THE--
CRUNCH
CHEEP

CONTINUE WATCHING?
It's been, like, 8 hours. Don't you have obligations?
I'm pretty sure you need a shower, at least.

TOUCHÉ.

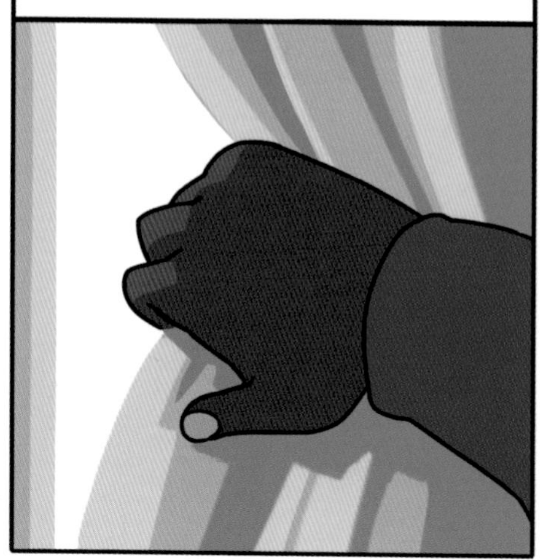
TWO DAYS WITHOUT ANY MONSTERS AND TWO DECADES OF VAMPIRE CLASSICS DOWN...

MIGHT BE TIME TO QUIT HIDING AND FACE REALITY.
FWIFFF

MAYBE I *DID* MAKE IT ALL UP.
OOF, IT SURE IS DAYTIME.

IN YOU GO. MIGHT AS WELL CHECK ON KAREN, SEE IF I STILL HAVE A JOB.

PLUS, THIS GUY NEEDS A REAL TANK. UP FOR A TRIP, SILAS?
Murder,

THE WAY I SEE IT IS THIS:

I'M PRETTY SURE IT ALL HAPPENED. THE LIGHTS, THE EXPLOSION, THE SPOOKY ABSCENCE-OF-LIGHT ALIEN IN A SUIT.

THE SPARKS COMING OUT OF MY HANDS.
THE...GOLDFISH?

IT'S FUNNY. YOU CAN BELIEVE SOMETHING SO HARD AND THEN AS SOON AS SOMEONE PUTS THE LITTLEST DOUBT IN YOUR MIND...
...YOU START TO WONDER, WAS IT REAL?

IN THIS CASE, AND I'M NOT SURE WHY, BUT...
CUTE

...I KINDA HOPE IT WAS.
·Maple Dr
BUS STOP
PARK!

LATERS

GREAT.
HEY, EXCUSE ME, SORRY--IS THERE AN ACCIDENT?

NOT SURE. TRAFFIC'S BEEN BAD BUT WE AIN'T MOVIN' AT ALL.
IS IT OKAY IF I GET OFF? I'M RUNNING LATE.

CAN'T LET YOU OFF OUTSIDE A STOP, MA'AM. REGULATIONS.
ARE YOU SURE? IT'S JUST A HALF-BLOCK AND--
THWAK!
WHAH!

WHAT WAS THAT?

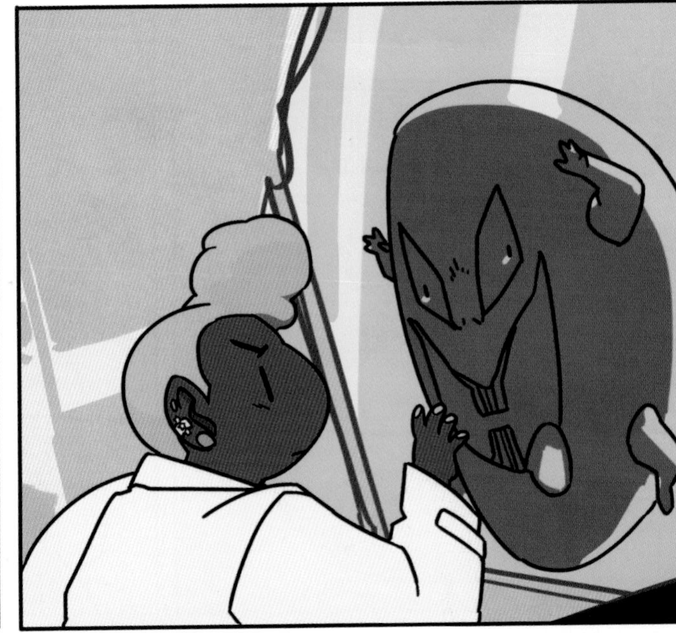

KABOOM

UUUGGGHH...

SILAS?
MISS? HEY, ARE YOU OKAY?

YOUR GOLDFISH, I THINK.
OH NO, HE'LL DRY OUT! IS THERE ANY WATER?

HERE. DARN KIDS, THROWING ROCKS THROUGH-- HEY, YOU HAVEN'T GOT A SCRATCH ON YOU!
I...OH, WEIRD. I DON'T?

THWAK!

DUCK!

WHO'S BLOWING UP MY BUS?
I DON'T KNOW!
WE'VE GOT TO GET OUT BEFORE THEY COME BACK!

STAY LOW!

AW, WHAT?!

NOT AGAIN.

HIT THE DECK!

WHA?

WOAH.
STAND BACK.

THEY'RE EVERYWHERE. GET OFF THE MAIN ROAD AND RUN.

NOT YOU.
WHO... WHO ARE YOU?
SCAMPER

KEVIN. YOU FELT THAT LIGHT, DIDN'T YOU? FROM NOWHERE, AND THEN EVERYTHING WAS DIFFERENT.

EXACTLY.
IT WASN'T JUST YOU.

WELL, YEAH, I--HEY, WAIT. WAIT! YOU'RE THE CONSTRUCTION GUY! YOU WAVED AT ME!

OH, WOAH. SO I DID.
I LIKED YOUR HAIR.

AAAH!

HOW DID YOU DO THAT?
I'M NOT REALLY SURE. YOU CAN'T?

I FRIGGIN' WISH.

INCOMING.

TAKE THAT!

JERKS.

WOW.

NO SWIRLY MYSTICAL LIGHT BEAMS, EITHER?
NO. NOT REALLY. NOT EVEN CLOSE, ACTUALLY.

DO YOU MIND... CAN I ASK YOU A QUESTION?
LET ME GUESS.

UM... WHAT'S WITH THE OUTFIT?

IT'S MY ARMOR.

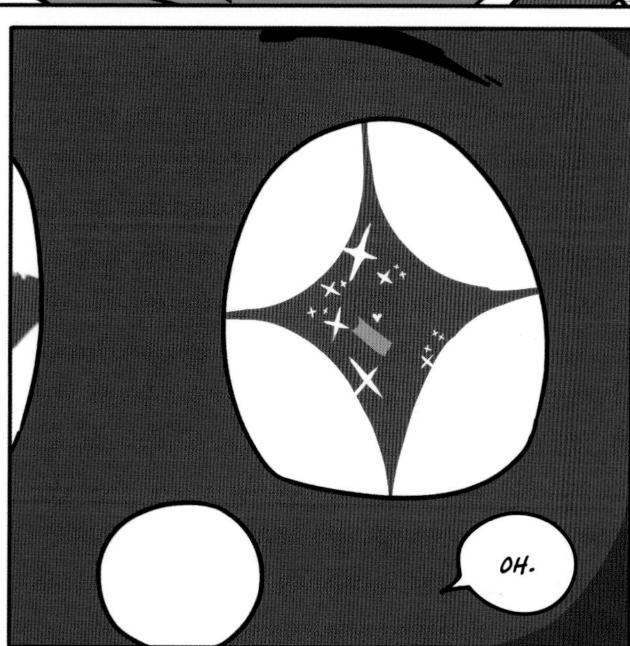
OH.

WATCH YOUR HEADS!

HAH!

THERE ARE MORE?
DUDE.

ABOUT A DOZEN. NOT FAR OFF. AT LEAST THEY BLOW UP EASY?
DUDE.

AMIE, RIGHT? I SAW YOU ON TV. I WAS ON MY WAY TO FIND YOU AND THEN...THIS.

I'M KEVIN. ALSO STRUCK BY WEIRD ALIEN MAGIC.
SANDY. NICE TO MEET YOU.

UH, HEY.

THIS IS SILAS. HE'S A GOLDFISH.
WHAT DOES HE DO?
THE ANSWER MAY SURPRISE YOU.

WELL, IT LOOKS LIKE I CAN FLY AND PUNCH STUFF.
AMIE?
I...I HAVE WEIRD... SPARKS. SOME KIND OF ENERGY, I THINK. IT ONLY HAPPENED ONCE.

OH, AND I KEEP GETTING CUTS AND THEN THEY VANISH, KAPOOF.
JUST OUT OF CURIOSITY, DID NEITHER OF YOU GET A COSTUME?

DID YOU?

SO...WE'RE ALL...MAGIC?

SURE LOOKS THAT WAY.
WE'RE GOING TO NEED IT. LOOK ALIVE!
STOP

IT'S COOL. I'LL CATCH UP.

HUH?!

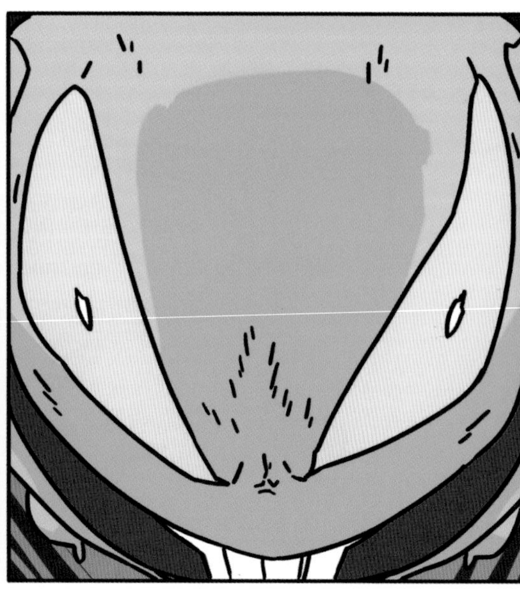

STOP!
?
!
AAAH!
GET AWAY!

HAT'S BEEN UT IN MOTION.
EY WILL FIND YOU, ALL OF YOU.

THEY WILL TAKE BACK WHAT YOU STOLE.
YOU NEED TO STEP OFF!

SILAS!

OW.

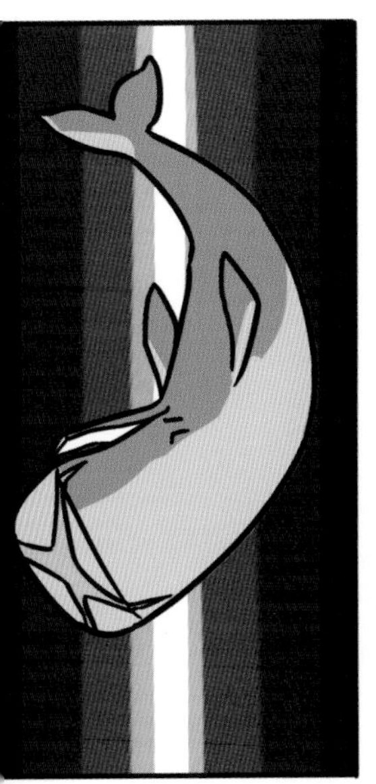

SBLOOP!

HOLY CROW. WAS THAT YOU?
NOT THE WHOLE TIME.
THAT WAS INCREDIBLE! GOLDFISH SAVES THE DAY!

TOLD YOU YOU'D BE SURPRISED.
YOU HAVE A TINY LASER WHALE? WHY DID YOU NOT LEAD WITH "I HAVE A TINY LASER WHALE?!"
HE'S SO CUTE!

CLIK!
CLIK
CLIK!
CLIK!
CLIK
CLIK!
CLIK
CLIK!

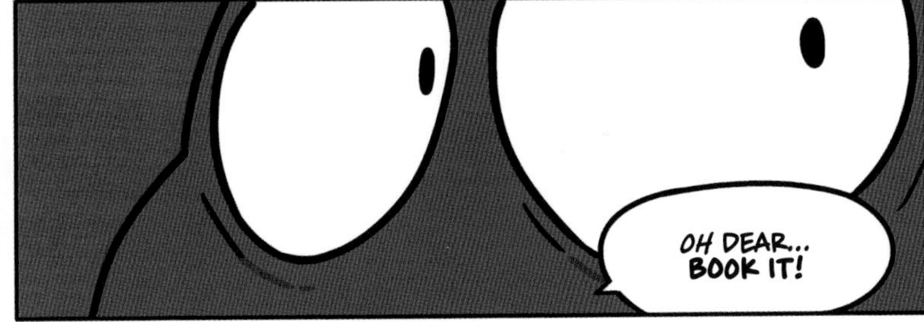
OH DEAR... BOOK IT!

TO THE SANDYMOBILE!

PHEW, WE SHOULD BE FAR ENOUGH TO SLOW DOWN.
CAN I START ASKING IF EITHER OF YOU HAVE ANY IDEA WHAT'S GOING ON?

WISH I DID, KIDDO. THIS IS ALL NEW TO ME, TOO.
KIDDO?! I'M PRETTY SURE I'M OLDER THAN YOU.

WELL, I'M OLDEST, SO I GET FIRST QUESTION. AMIE, DO YOU REMEMBER MEETING ME AT THE PET STORE?

OH, OH! THE CRICKET LADY!
EXACTLY. THE LIGHT HIT ME RIGHT AFTER I LEFT, SO I THOUGHT MAYBE YOU HAD SOMETHING TO DO WITH IT.

NOPE. I GOT ATTACKED, BUT SILAS SAVED ME.
THAT'S A GOOD PET, THAT IS.

I WAS ON MY WAY TO DROP THESE TWO OFF AND THEN I WAS GOING TO COME FIND YOU. SUDDENLY, KAPOW!

THESE WHO?

HEY.
UH, HI?

AMIE, KEVIN, THESE ARE MY KIDS, CECILY AND LUKE.

HEY.
I LIKE YOUR OUTFIT.

WE NEED TO GET SECRET IDENTITIES.

CHAPTER THREE

WHAT ABOUT SOMETHING LIKE... SUPER MOM?

SEEMS A LITTLE OBVIOUS.
FWEEEEEEE

THE...FLYING... PUNCH...LADY?

MIGHT BE TRICKY TO FIT ON THE COSTUME, BUT I LIKE THE SIMPLICITY.
MILK, KEVIN?

YES, PLEASE!
THIS IS HARDER THAN IT LOOKS.

MAYBE WE SHOULD BACKTRACK A LITTLE BEFORE WE COME UP WITH OUR NAMES, HMM?

I'D PERSONALLY LIKE TO KNOW WHY OUR MOM HAS SUPERPOWERS NOW.
OH YEAH, IT'S TOTALLY RAD.
NOT THAT IT ISN'T RAD.

THANK YOU, HON.
I'M JUST SAYING.

PLEASE DON'T PUT THIS ON THE INTERNET.
WELL, DUH.

SHE'S GOT A POINT. WHERE DO WE EVEN START? DID ANYBODY GET, LIKE, A MANUAL?

TING!
THE RATS' NEST
THE RATS' NEST
CA-CLICK!

--THEN I WENT TO PICK UP A CARTON OF EGGS AND THEY POPPED LIKE SOAP BUBBLES.

"I'M STILL WORKING ON IT, BUT I THINK MY BODY'S ADAPTING."

HOW DID YOU FIGURE OUT YOU COULD FLY?
OH!

"I WAS OUT FOR A JOG AND I TRIPPED. I JUST KEPT...FLOATING. AFTER THAT I KIND OF...KNEW, YOU KNOW?"

I AM SO MAD THAT IT'S NOT GENETIC.
THAT YOU KNOW OF.

WHAT ABOUT YOU?
WELL...

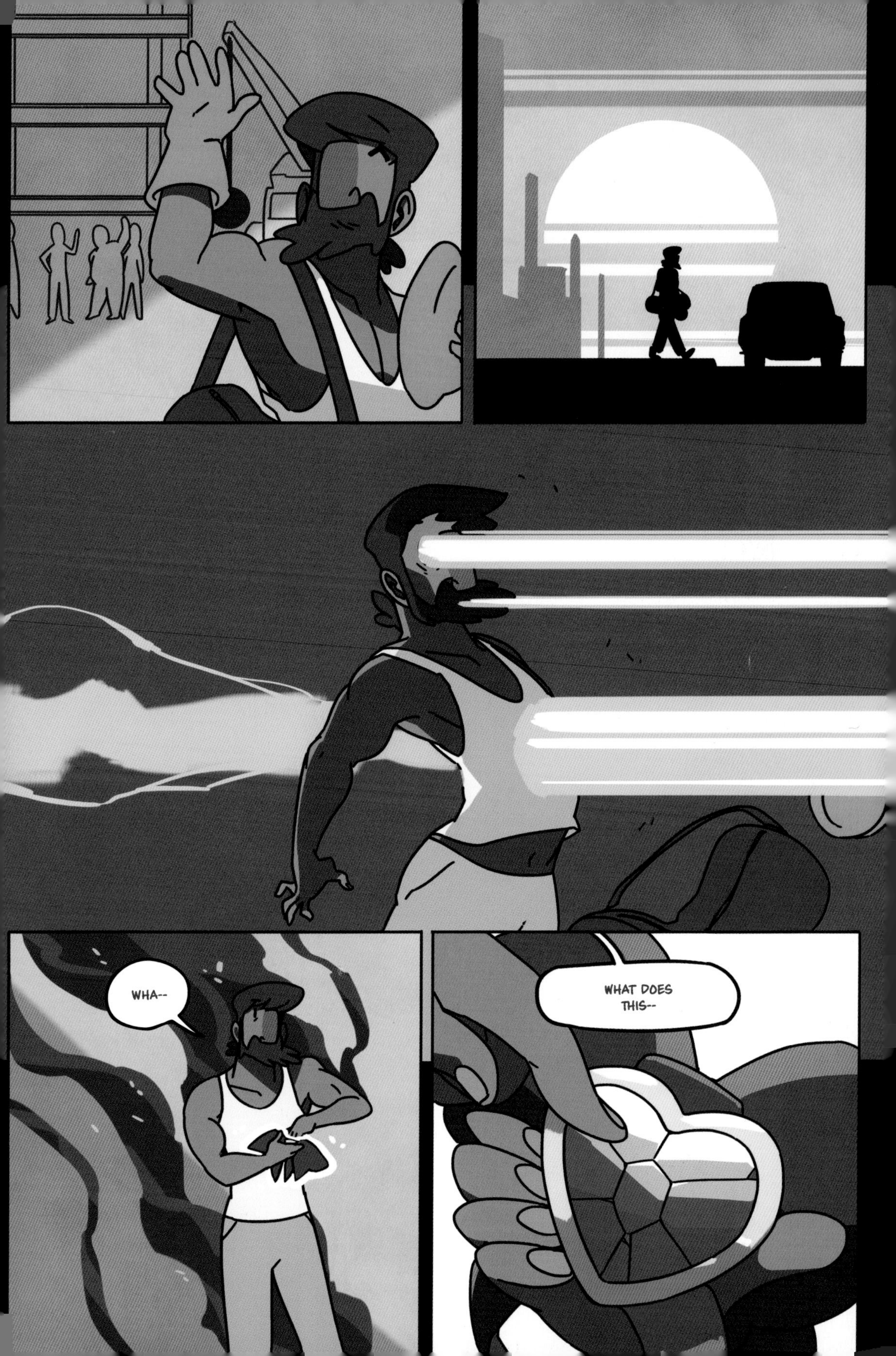
WHA--
WHAT DOES
THIS--

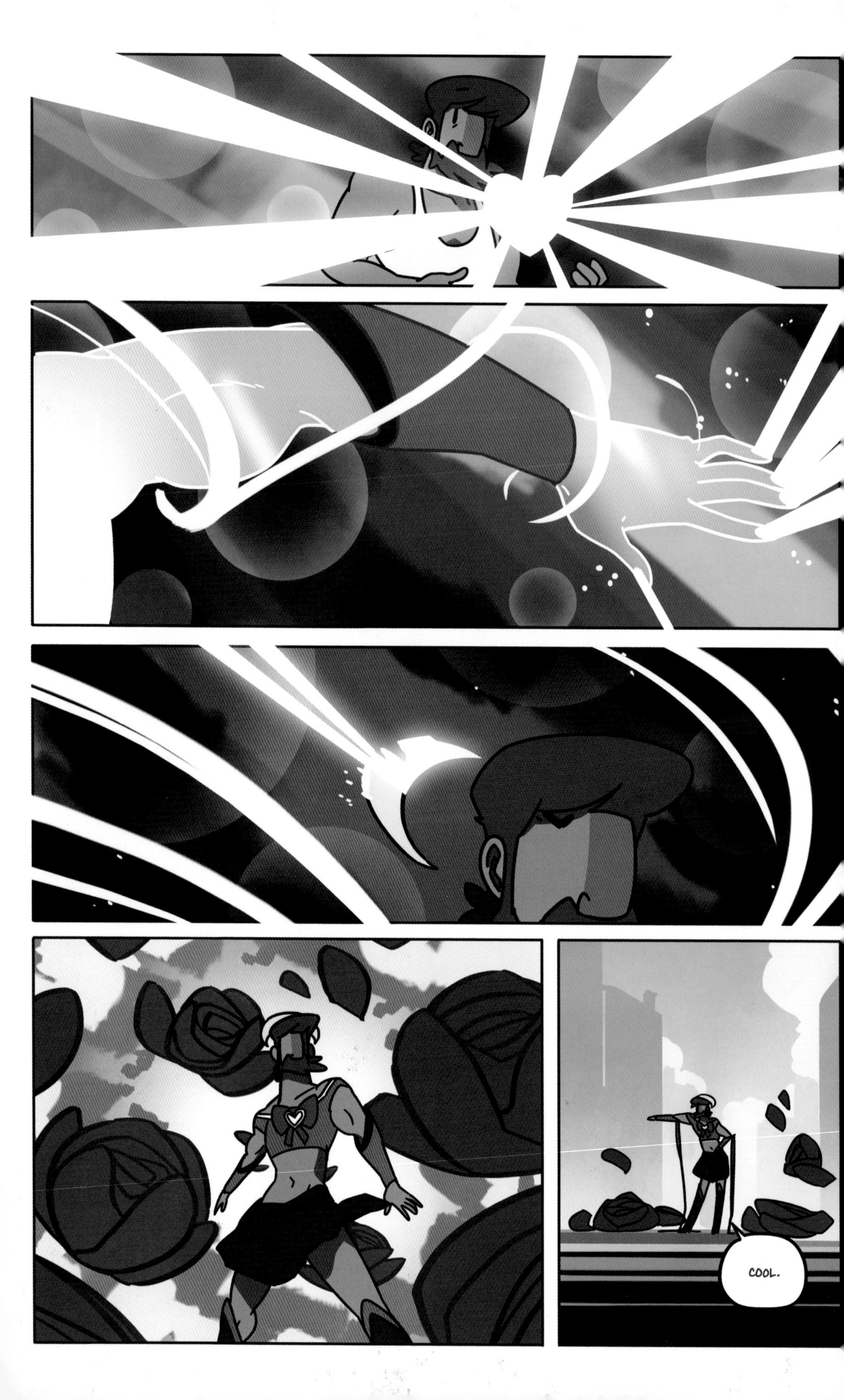
COOL.

AWESOME.

SO THE LOCKET... IT'S HOW YOU TRANSFORM.
WELL, YEAH, THE FIRST TIME.

NOW IT SEEMS TO HAPPEN WHENEVER I KNOW I NEED IT TO. I JUST WISH I COULD FIGURE OUT WHERE THE "UNDO" KEY IS.
HUH?

"IT DOESN'T WORK IN REVERSE. PLUS, THE COSTUME SEEMS TO APPEAR FROM WHEREVER I LEFT IT LAST, TRADING OUT WITH WHAT I'M WEARING."

SWITCHEROO, LIKE.

...AND IF, SAY, I LEFT IT AT HOME BEFORE I GOT INTO A SURPRISE BATTLE ON THE HIGHWAY...
GOTCHA.
FWEEEEEEEE

SO WE'RE ALL EQUALLY CONFUSED. THAT'S SOMEHOW REASSURING.

TEA, AMIE? SORRY, THOUGHT I HAD ENOUGH WATER BEFORE.
OH, NO WORRIES! HERBAL, IF YOU'VE GOT IT. THANKS!

IT'S HARD NOT TO WONDER WHY US, YOU KNOW?
OH, CAREFUL. IT'S HOT.

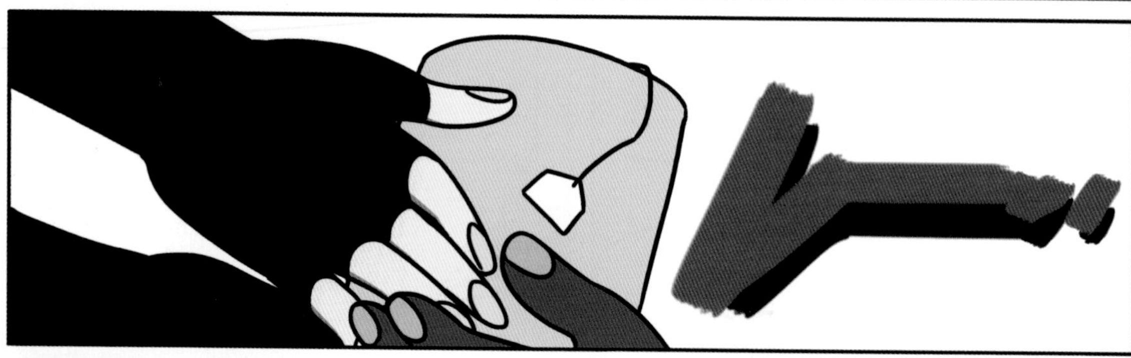

CRASH!

BLOOP

OKAY, WHAT?
AW, TEA.

NOT ON THE INTERNET!
UH HUH.
CLICK
CLICK
CLICK
CLICK
CLICK

YOU ARE ONE RESILIENT LITTLE DUDE, SILAS.

MY TABLE.
DID YOU DO THAT?
I DON'T... DID I?

WE OUGHTTA GET A LID FOR THAT THING.
WHAT HE NEEDS IS A REAL TANK.

CAN WE STOP AT MY CAR?

DING~!
!
COMING! SORRY, WE'RE NOT TECHNICALLY OPEN--
AAAAAAAA!
WHERE ARE THEY?!

WHAT ARE YOU?
THEY WERE HERE. I CAN FEEL IT.

TWO OF THEM. HEART AND SIGHT...

I DON'T KNOW WHAT YOU'RE TALKING ABOUT! *OH* GOD, DON'T KILL ME!
YOU DON'T KNOW.

WAIT.

THEY COME FOR YOU.

SO IT'S LIKE, WHY EVEN MAKE A SEQUEL, YOU KNOW?
TING
OH MAN, THE WORST!
JUST TRY

!!!
HAH!

WHAM
GIVE IT BACK.

IT IS NOT YOURS TO TAKE. NONE OF YOU.

GRAAAHHK!
BZZZZZZ

GRAHH!
CRASH

WE'VE GOT TO GET HIM OFF THE STREET!
YEAH, THIS NEVER GOES WELL FOR BUILDINGS IN THE MOVIES.

CAN WE FLY OUT? LURE HIM TO THE PARK?
WE CAN TRY!

HOLD ON TIGHT.

WOAH.

NO!

I DON'T THINK SO!

AAAAAAAHHH!
WHEEE-HAW!

KEVIN!

GOTCHA.

CRAAAH!
VOOM

UP AHEAD! BRACE YOURSELVES!
WHAT?!

SLAM

OW.
IT WASN'T ON PURPOSE! I'M NOT USUALLY THAT--

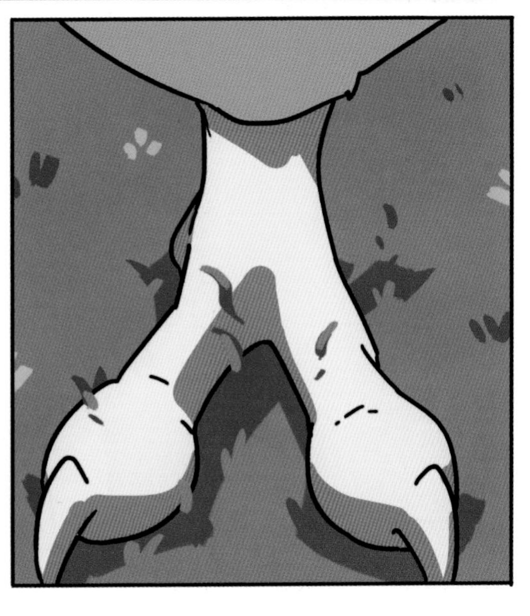

YOU FUMBLE BLINDLY WITH STOLEN MAGIC. LET ME RELIEVE YOU OF THE BURDEN.

I DON'T... I DON'T THINK SO?
YEAH, WE'RE GOOD.

THIS PATHETIC CREATURE DOES NOT DESERVE THE SIGHT. HOW CAN ANY OF YOU EVEN HOPE TO--
THAT'S MY FRIEND, YOU JERK!

IT IS A *FISH*.

HE'S **OUR** FISH.

WHAP!
OH, COME ON!

HUP!

WHA-BOOM!

!

HOW...

OH, CURDS!

IN YOU GO!

PHEW~

"SO, NOW DO YOU BELIEVE ME?"

I...I HONESTLY DON'T KNOW.

THERE'S A LOT OF THAT GOING AROUND.
UH HUH.

I WASN'T LYING. WHATEVER HAPPENED HERE--THE LIGHT, THAT ATTACK--IT WASN'T HUMAN.
UH HUH...

IT'S TRUE. SOMETHING HAPPENED TO ALL OF US.
HI, I'M KEVIN.
HUH.

AMIE?
YEAH?

YOU'RE FIRED.

FIRED!
I KNOW, SWEET-HEART.

I WENT TO ART SCHOOL. DO YOU HAVE ANY IDEA HOW MUCH DEBT I'M IN?
AND THAT'S WHY I SKIPPED COLLEGE.

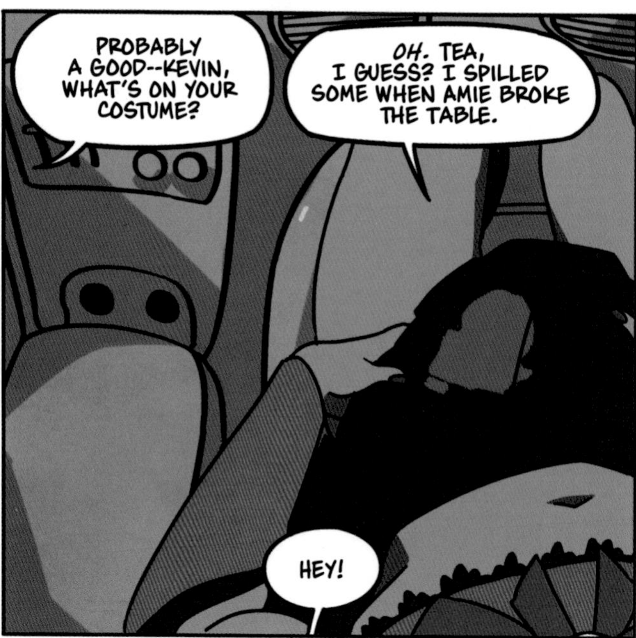
PROBABLY A GOOD--KEVIN, WHAT'S ON YOUR COSTUME?
OH. TEA, I GUESS? I SPILLED SOME WHEN AMIE BROKE THE TABLE.
HEY!

CHECK IN THAT BACK POCKET ON YOUR LEFT. THERE SHOULD BE A BLEACH PEN.
UH, OKAY.
IT'S NOT THAT BAD.

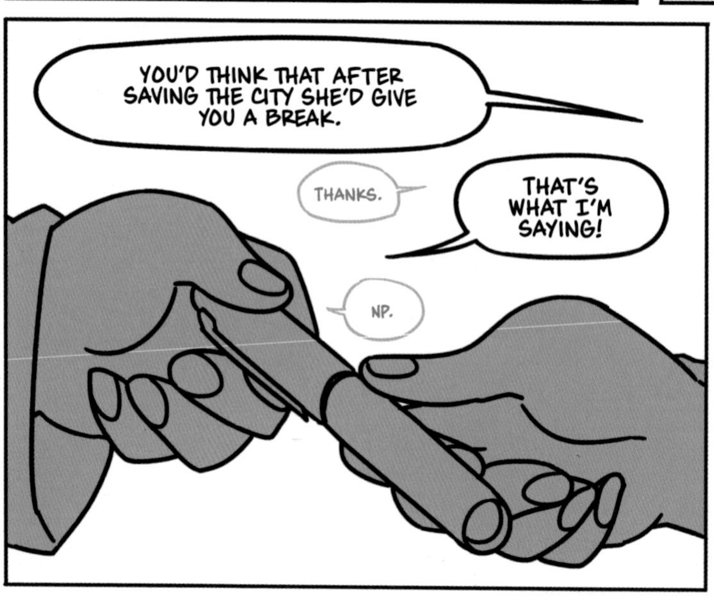
YOU'D THINK THAT AFTER SAVING THE CITY SHE'D GIVE YOU A BREAK.
THANKS.
THAT'S WHAT I'M SAYING!
NP.

OUR LIVES ARE GOING TO GET KIND OF MESSY, AREN'T THEY?

NEED ANY HELP?
NAH, I SHOULD BE ALRIGHT. THANKS FOR THE LIFT!

HUH. STAIRS.

SOMEONE GOT A RAISE.
SOMEONE USED HER FORBIDDEN CREDIT CARD.

MATTER OF FACT, THAT SAME SOMEONE GOT FIRED TODAY FOR SAVING THE WORLD.
YEAH, I HEARD ABOUT THAT.

WAIT--YOU WHAT? HEARD ABOUT-- WHERE?!

INTERNET.

MOM.

JUST SO YOU KNOW, IT WASN'T US.
HON, CAN YOU COME IN HERE?

OH, YOU'RE HOME.
YEAH.

CHANNEL 4
NEWS

OH. THAT.

WE SHOULD TALK.

CHAPTER FOUR

It's not the pale mo
WE GOT SOME OF AMIE'S MAIL AGAIN. THAT GIRL...
excites me~

rills and delights me~
TURN IT UP, WILL YA?

DARN TOOTIN'.
BLECH!

YOU'RE THE BOSS.

I KNOW YOU LOVE ME!
COME BACK WHEN YOU DON'T STINK LIKE A HOT SUMMER DUMPSTER, AND WE'LL TALK.
AMIE BLOOM

SO, HOW'D IT GO?
IN A WORD?

PBBBBLLLLTT.
OUCH.
THE TALE OF ELF-O
RUMBLE
RUMBLE
RUMBL

THAT BAD, *HUH?*
THE WORST.
I DON'T KNOW HOW A GUY CAN BE MAD THAT HIS SUPER COOL WIFE JUST ALSO HAPPENS TO BE ABLE TO FLY.

COOL? *HAH.* YOU THINK?
FROSTY.

I THINK HE WAS MORE UPSET ABOUT FINDING OUT FROM THE NEWS INSTEAD OF ME, BUT WHAT WAS I SUPPOSED TO SAY, YOU KNOW? "HI, YES, THESE TWO STRANGERS AND I HAVE MAGICAL ABILITIES. ALSO, THE GOLDFISH SHOOTS LASERS."
WOULD'VE BEEN NICE IF ALL THIS CAME WITH A WALKTHROUGH, THAT'S FOR SURE.
"HOW TO TELL YOUR HUSBAND YOU CAN PUNCH THROUGH STEEL, AND OTHER HELPFUL TIPS FOR THE NEWLY SUPERHUMAN."
KEVIN! YOU DID A JOKE!
PERISH THE THOUGHT.
IT'LL BE ALRIGHT, THOUGH. WE'LL BE ALRIGHT. THERE ARE MORE IMPORTANT ISSUES TO DEAL WITH FIRST.
THE ALIENS?
COSTUMES? NICKNAMES? WHY MY POWERS DON'T MAKE ANY SENSE?
KEVIN, YOUR APARTMENT IS DISGUSTING.
TO BE FAIR...IT'S ACTUALLY A GARAGE.

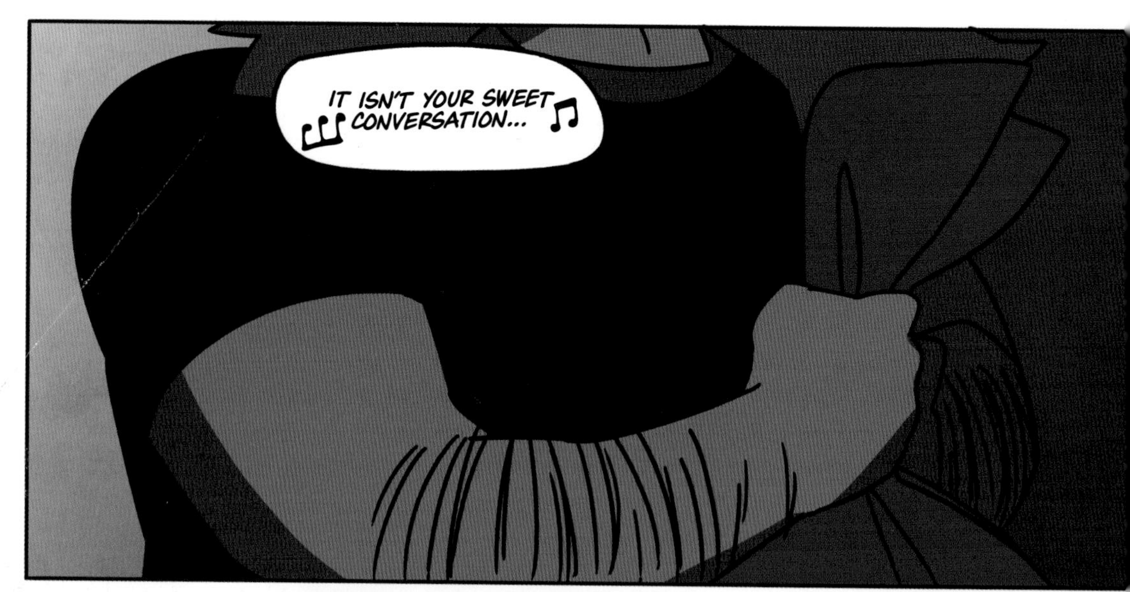
IT ISN'T YOUR SWEET CONVERSATION...

...THAT BRINGS THIS SENSATION!

...OHHH NO, IT'S JUST THE NEARNESS OF--

WOOOSH

HOW MANY MVP TROPHIES DO YOU HAVE IN HERE, KEV? FRIG DANG!
KEV'S STUFF
TROPHIES 2010-2011
COOL TAPES

HAH! A FEW, I GUESS. I WAS A GOALIE RIGHT THROUGH TO MY SECOND CRACK AT SENIOR YEAR.
IT'S HARD TO IMAGINE YOU AS A JOCK.

REALLY A STRETCH, AMIE.

OOH, HERE SHE IS! THE CREAM O' THE CROP, TOP O' THE HEAP!

LADY BEATRICE ALCATRAZ!

BZZZZZZZZZZT

YOU KNOW, LIKE THE PRISON, BECAUSE YOU CAN'T ESCAPE IT.
NO, I GET THAT PART--

UM, KEVIN? DID YOU PUT YOUR COSTUME IN THE WASH?
YEP. STILL WON'T CLEAN ITSELF.

DID YOU PUT IT IN WITH YOUR WHITES?

OH, WHAT?!
IT'S BRIGHT RED! YOU CAN'T MIX LOADS LIKE THAT!
I DIDN'T KNOW! IT WAS DIRTY!
KEVIN.
BRRING!

YYYELLO, AMIE HERE.

AMIE, ARE YOU HOME?

WHY ARE YOU YELLING? ARE YOU LOCKED OUT AGAIN?
NOT EXACTLY.

I NEED YOUR HELP, LIKE RIGHT NOW.
ARE YOU OKAY?

YOU REMEMBER WHEN YOU SAID ON TV HOW THAT LIGHT HIT YOU, AND THEN EVERYTHING CHANGED, AND YOU THOUGHT MAYBE YOU WERE CRAZY AND NOBODY BELIEVED YOU?

WELL, ABOUT THAT--

I DO. I BELIEVE.
SAL...

PEEK-A-BOO.

I SEE YOU.
AAAH!
DON'T RUN FROM ME, DARLING. WE HAVE SO MUCH TO DISCUSS!
YOU'RE NOT HIM! PUT ME DOWN!
SAL! SAL?

LET GO OF ME, YOU--
SAL!

I'M NOT DOING YOUR LAUNDRY FOR YOU, YOU'RE A GROWN MAN!
NOBODY ASKED YOU TO! I JUST DON'T SEE--
YOU GUYS!

I THINK MY NEIGHBOR'S IN TROUBLE.
RUMMAGE
RUMMAGE
RUMMAGE
HOLD ON.

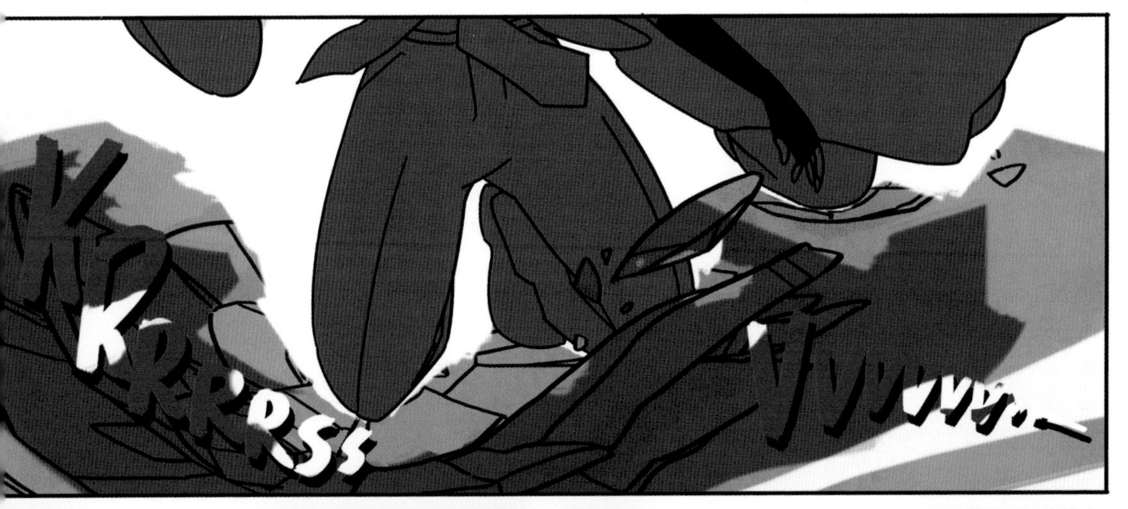
KRRRSS
VVVVVV

SAL! SAL!

COME ON, BE OKAY! SAL! DEREK!
CRASH

THROUGH HERE!
BUMP!
CE CREAM
SORRY

OH, GOOD. YOU GOT MY TEXT.
HOOOOLY SNAKES.

JUST KIDDING. HI, THOUGH. GLAD YOU COULD MAKE IT.
ALRIGHT THEN.
GOOD TALK.
JUMP!
KRATHOOM
KRATHOOM
AAAAHAHAHA!

WHA?

DEREK, PLEASE! BABY, STOP THIS!
UGH, "BABY?"

LISTEN, KITTEN-PANTS, YOUR HUBBY SCOOCHED OVER AND I'M DRIVING. IF YOUR FRIENDS GIVE ME WHAT I WANT, YOU GET HIM BACK. CAPEESH?
DEREK...

YOU HEAR THAT, HUMANS? THESE POWERS DON'T BELONG TO YOU. IT'S NOT NICE TO TAKE THINGS THAT AREN'T YOURS.

YOU'RE HURT!
HEALING POWERS. I'LL BE FINE. WE HAVE TO GET SILAS.
HOW?
MY APARTMENT. FLY UP AND OVER. BEDROOM WINDOW'S OPEN A CRACK.

WHAT ABOUT YOU TWO?
I'VE GOT KEVIN.
I'VE GOT AMIE.
OKAY. IN THREE, TWO--

NOW!
RIGHT.

YOU'RE THE SPIRIT?

HAH!

AWW, DAMP.
KEVIN, LOOK OUT!

YOU CLOD! THESE GIFTS ARE WASTED ON YOU!
SWIPE!
NOT THE FIRST TIME I'VE HEARD THAT, YOU KNOW...

STINGS A LITTLE LESS THESE DAYS!
DON'T HURT HIM!

HE'S STILL IN THERE! POSSESSED OR, OR POISONED, OR SOMETHING, BUT HE'S MY DEREK!

COME ON, SANDY, COME ON...

NONE OF YOU UNDERSTAND. WE WAITED MILLIONS OF YEARS FOR THAT STAR TO DIE! *MILLIONS!*
THAT SOUNDS LIKE... SOME INEFFECTIVE... TIME MANAGEMENT.

KEVIN!
AW, SHE MISSES YOU.

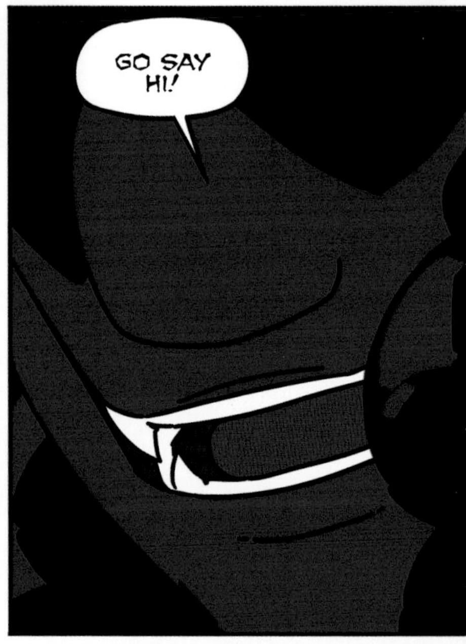
GO SAY HI!

AUGH... I'M...SORRY...

IT'S OKAY. I KEEP TELLING YOU...

HEALING POWERS.

DO YOU THINK--
NO IDEA. LET'S TRY IT.

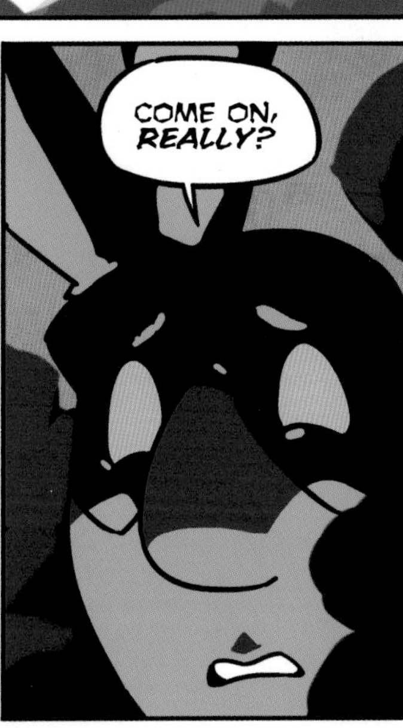
COME ON, *REALLY?*

GO, LADY BEATRICE!
DEREK!
YAAAUUGGHH!

WUH-OH.

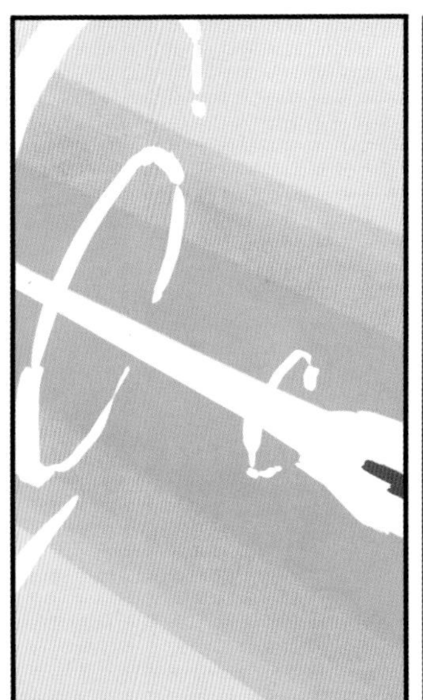

GOTCHA!
ERP!

DEREK. DEREK. WAKE UP!

IS HE OKAY?
DEREK, BABE, PLEASE. TALK TO ME. BE OKAY.

WOOO, BE CAREFUL WITH THAT.

AH! YOU'RE AWAKE!
MMMM. WHAT'D I MISS?

...IT HAD MY NAME ON IT?
MMHMM. NO ADDRESS, THOUGH. IT WASN'T EVEN SEALED.

THAT THING FELL OUT, AND AS SOON AS I TOUCHED IT--
KAPOW.
EXACTLY. IT TOOK OVER. I COULD SEE WHAT WAS HAPPENING, BUT...

I'M SORRY I SCARED YOU.
IT'S OKAY. IT'S FINE, OF COURSE IT'S FINE. IT WASN'T YOU.

HOW DID YOU DO IT? THAT ATTACK, YOUR HEALING POWERS--HOW?
I'M NOT REALLY SURE. WE JUST TOUCHED, AND WHEN WE GRABBED LADY--
GEOFFREY.
PROZZÄK

HUH?
THE STAFF. I NAMED IT GEOFFREY. GEOFF, FOR SHORT.

TO ANSWER YOUR QUESTION, SANDY, I DON'T KNOW, BUT WE WERE OUT OF OPTIONS AND TIME.

OH YEAH, WHAT HAPPENED? WHERE WERE YOU?

I COULDN'T FIND A CLEAN CUP.

SORRY.
IT'S ALRIGHT. YOU CAUGHT US.

THANK YOU, ALL OF YOU. I THINK HE NEEDS SOME REST, AND YOU'VE PROBABLY GOT A LOT TO TALK ABOUT.
I'M FINE...
I'LL DROP OFF THE CLOTHES TOMORROW AND CHECK UP ON YOU.

KEVIN...?
YEAH?
PROZZÄK

PLEASE DON'T WASH... THEM WITH...YOUR COSTUME...

A BLACK HOLE IN A SUIT, A BUNCH OF EXPLODING BUBBLEGUM CREEPS, A GRYPHON-WOMAN, AND NOW A SURPRISE POSSESSION.
I'LL HAND IT TO WHOEVER'S AFTER US, THEY'RE NOT BORING.

YOU MISSED A GOOD ONE, BUDDY.
I SUPPOSE IT WOULDN'T HAVE DONE MUCH GOOD--I DOUBT WE COULD'VE ZAPPED OR PUNCHED THAT THING OUT OF DEREK WITHOUT HURTING HIM.
NEXT BATTLE, SILAS. ALL LASER WHALE, ALL THE TIME.
I KEEP HOPING THIS WILL START TO MAKE SENSE, BUT MAYBE I SHOULD JUST ROLL WITH IT.
BET YOU WISH YOU HAD MY BOOK RIGHT ABOUT NOW.
THERE IT IS AGAIN! JOKESTER KEVIN, FIRING OFF A MILE A MINUTE!
PROZZÄK
IT WOULD BE NICE TO HAVE SOME ANSWERS, THAT'S FOR SURE.

CHAPTER FIVE

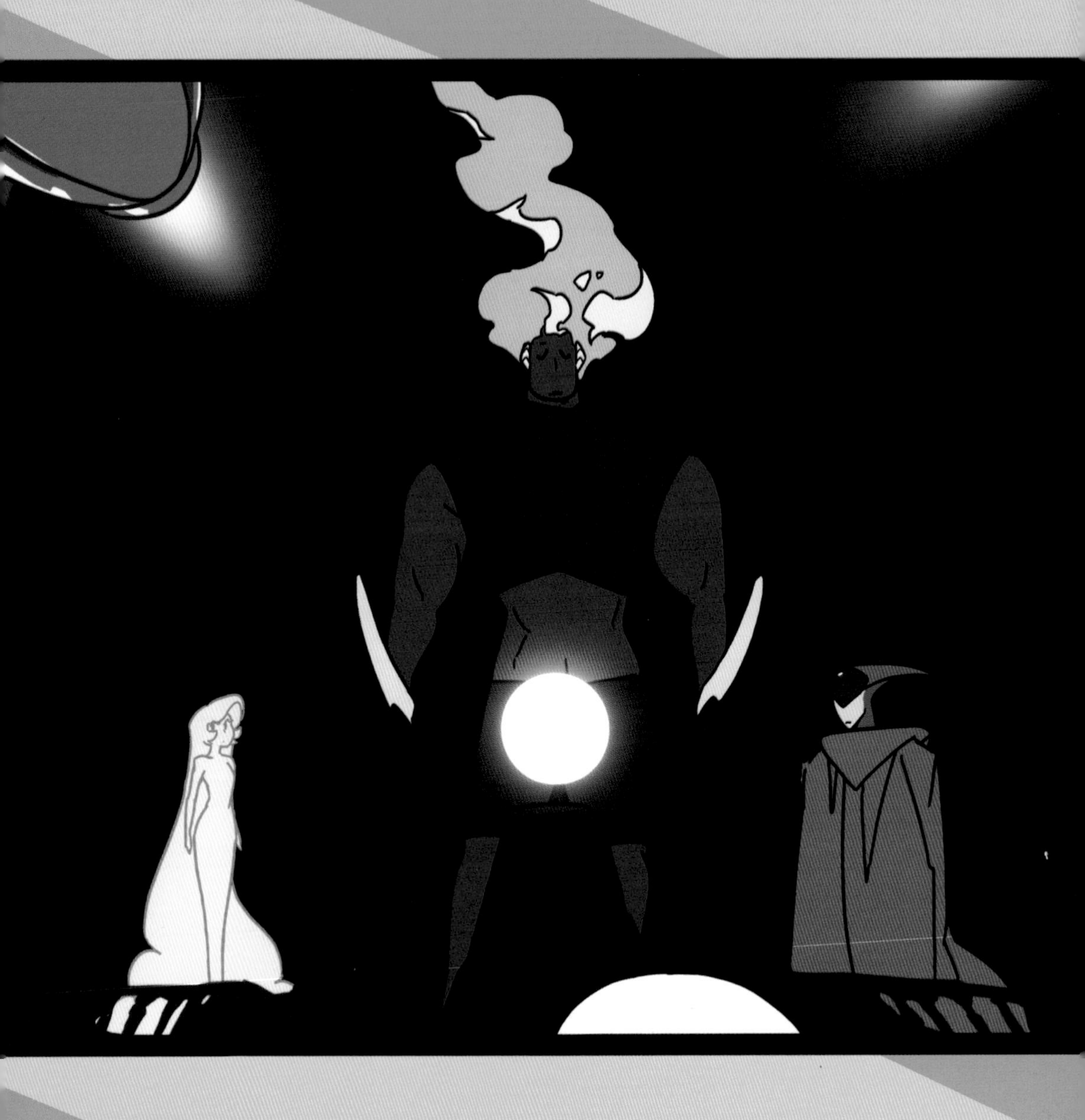

WHEN THEY FIRST LOOKED UP AND BEGAN TO CHART THE SKIES, THEY PREDICTED:

"A STAR WILL DIE AS ANOTHER IS BORN, AND SO WILL THEY BE CHOSEN.

"FOUR WARRIORS TO CHAMPION US INTO A NEW AGE--A TIME OF PEACE.

"OF STRENGTH.

"OF CELEBRATION.

SANDY
AMIE
"IN THE OLDEST LANGUAGE, BY THE WISEST HANDS, IT WAS WRITTEN."

TWO WEEKS AGO:

PLACES, EVERYONE!

ANY MINUTE NOW.
HOW ARE WE SUPPOSED TO KNOW IF IT'S WORKING?
IT'LL... I DON'T KNOW, IT'LL GLOW OR SOMETHING, WON'T IT?
FOCUS. A HUNDRED WORLDS HAVE EYES ON US. BE READY.

CAN YOU... DO YOU SEE ANYTHING?
NOT YET.

QUIT WHISPERING, YOU TWO!
ARE WE DOING THIS RIGHT? THE HEART ISN'T MOVING, OR... DOING ANYTHING, REALLY.

MAYBE THERE'S SOME KIND OF DELAY. IT'S BILLIONS OF LIGHTYEARS AWAY, AFTER ALL...

NOX. WHAT'S HAPPENING?
OH, CREPES.

I DON'T KNOW, ZILLAH. IT'S LATE.
THAT'S IMPOSSIBLE. YOU SAID THE PROPHECY LEFT NO ROOM FOR ERROR.
I KNOW WHAT I SAID, Z.
IS THAT THE CAPTAIN?
IT'S NOT BUZZING, OR EXPLODING, OR WHATEVER IT'S SUPPOSED TO DO.
DON'T POKE IT, UNA!
NOX...THEY'RE LEAVING.
WHAT?
THE WARSHIPS. THE SATELLITES, THE SCOUTS... THEY'RE WARPING OUT.
THE HAETHRON LEFT, AND THE FLEET OF THE UNHOLY. EVEN GRYPHON'S OUT OF ORBIT.
NOTHING'S HAPPENED YET. WHY WOULD THEY LEAVE?

UNA! THE CAMERAS!
STAY HERE IF YOU WANT, PRUE. I'M GOING TO SEE WHAT THE HOLDUP IS.
THEY'RE GONE.
END

WHO'S GONE?
THE ALIENS. THE WARSHIPS. ALL THE TROOPS WAITING TO ATTACK AFTER THE OCCURRENCE--THEY'VE LEFT OUR AIRSPACE.
WHAT?
NOX, WHAT'S GOING ON? THE HEART ISN'T WORKING. HOW LONG HAS IT BEEN?
T-TWELVE MINUTES...
WE'VE BEEN WAITING THREE THOUSAND YEARS, UNA. WHAT'S ANOTHER HALF HOUR?

NO, SHE'S RIGHT. THE PREDICTIONS WERE EXACT. IT SHOULD'VE STARTED BY NOW.
COULD THEY, PERHAPS, HAVE BEEN MISINTERPRETED?
I HIGHLY DOUBT IT, ROWAN.

"A STAR SHALL DIE AS ANOTHER IS BORN, AND SO SHALL THEY BE CHOSEN.

"THREE WARRIORS TO LEAD US INTO A NEW AGE--A TIME OF PROSPERITY."
WE'VE HAD THIS MEMORIZED SINCE WE WERE EIGHTY. YOU RECITED IT AT OUR WEDDING. WE KNOW.
THAT WAS A LITTLE TACKY.

"OF POWER AND REVELRY."

"STRENGTH, SPIRIT, AND SIGHT WILL GATHER TO THEIR HEART, WHICH WILL EMPOWER THEM ALL."
YEAH, BUT THE HEART DIDN'T EMPOWER, AND NONE OF US CHANGED.

WHAT DO WE EVEN DO NOW?
DING DONG

THERE'S SOME MISUNDERSTANDING. YOU'VE TRAINED FOR THIS ALL YOUR LIVES. THERE'S NOBODY ELSE--
NOX, COME IN. WE FOUND THEM.

FOUND WHO?

THE SHIPS. THEY'RE--EVERY SINGLE ONE OF THE DESTROYERS, SCAVENGERS AND MERCENARIES THAT HAVE BEEN IN OUR SKIES FOR MONTHS ARE HEADED TO THE SAME PLANET.

SUIT UP.

COORDINATES ARE SET. YOU SHOULD ARRIVE IN APPROXIMATELY THIRTEEN DAYS.
TWO WEEKS? THE HAETHRON WILL BE THERE IN SECONDS!
I KNOW, BUT NONE OF YOU CAN TELEPORT, AND THIS IS THE FASTEST BOAT WE'VE GOT.
ZILLAH...
YOU'LL STILL BEAT MOST OF THE WARSHIPS, AND OUR FLEET WILL BE CLOSE BEHIND. YOU'RE THE STRONGEST TEAM OF WARRIORS THIS SYSTEM HAS, POWERS OR NOT. WE NEED YOU.
I'LL RELAY INFORMATION AS WE INTERCEPT IT. GOOD LUCK.
I DON'T UNDERSTAND. WHY DIDN'T IT HAPPEN?
THIS TIMING CANNOT BE A COINCIDENCE. WHATEVER OCCURRED ON THE PLANET OUR ENEMIES ARE RACING TOWARDS...I SUSPECT WE'LL FIND OUR ANSWERS.
THEY'RE RIGHT, NOX. NONE OF US BLAME YOU. WE'LL FIGURE IT OUT.
IT'S JUST...I WAS SO SURE.
THAT'S THE THING ABOUT PROPHECIES, ISN'T IT?

LANGUAGE IS MUTABLE. THIS MEANS THAT OVER GENERATIONS IT CHANGES, ADAPTS, TAKES ON NEW MEANINGS.
THINK OF IT LIKE PLAYING TELEPHONE, BUT FOR THOUSANDS OF YEARS AND ACROSS VAST DISTANCES. THE MESSAGE EVOLVES.
PROJECT THEIR OWN BELIEFS AND EXPERIENCES ON WORDS AS THEY DECRYPT THEM, ALTERING THE STORY, MAKING IT WORK FOR THEIR NEEDS.
OTHERS SIMPLY...MISTRANSLATE.
STRENGTH MIGHT BE READ AS POWER. CELEBRATION, AS REVELRY.

A FOUR CAN LOOK AN AWFUL LOT LIKE A THREE.

BEFORE OUR PLANET WAS CONCEIVED, NOX WAS A GIRL OBSESSED WITH THE STORIES OF HER PEOPLE.
THE FIRST MYSTICS OF HER WORLD PREDICTED AN EVENT, AN OCCURRENCE, THAT WOULD GRANT ABILITIES TO THE THREE MOST WORTHY BY EMPOWERING AN OBJECT THEY CALLED
THE HEART.
THE WORDS WERE OLD WHEN SHE WAS YOUNG. SHE TAUGHT HERSELF DOZENS OF LANGUAGES IN ORDER TO READ THEM, TO SOLVE THEIR MYSTERY. WHEN SHE WAS SURE SHE'D PINPOINTED THE EXACT DATE IT WAS MEANT TO HAPPEN, SHE SET OUT.
SHE CROSSED THE GALAXY, SEEKING OUT THE CHOSEN FEW TO BE HER TRIO OF WARRIORS, PREPARING THEM FOR THEIR DESTINY.
THE STRENGTH WOULD BE A POWERHOUSE, A FIGHTER UNMATCHED IN BRAWN AND SKILL.
THE SPIRIT WOULD BE AGILE, GRACEFUL, BEAUTIFUL, AND DEADLY.
THE SIGHT WOULD HAVE KNOWLEDGE OF ALL THINGS, AND GUIDE THEM ALL IN THEIR JOURNEY.

THOUGH THEY IGNORED HER CLAIMS AT FIRST, NOX AND HER CREW OF ALIENS GREW FAMOUS, AND BEGAN ACQUIRING DEVOTED BELIEVERS. DOZENS OF WORLDS, IN HER SYSTEM AND BEYOND, WATCHED AND WAITED FOR THE MYSTERIOUS EVENT.

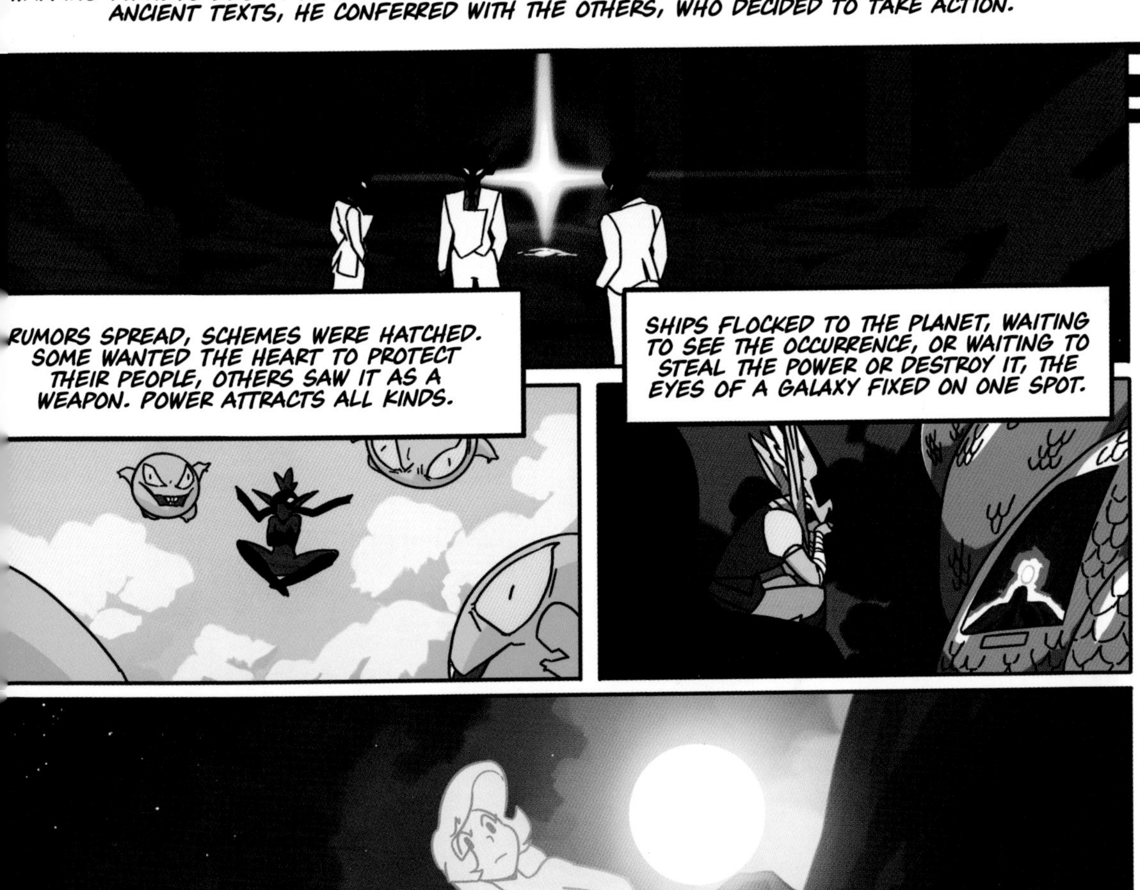

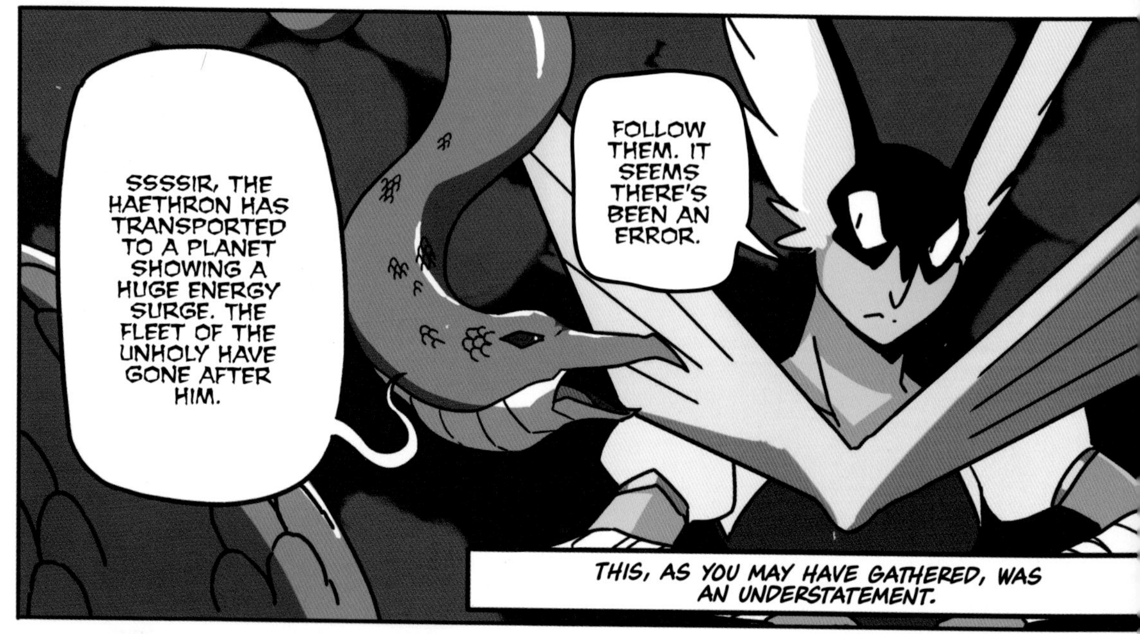
SSSSIR, THE HAETHRON HAS TRANSPORTED TO A PLANET SHOWING A HUGE ENERGY SURGE. THE FLEET OF THE UNHOLY HAVE GONE AFTER HIM.
FOLLOW THEM. IT SEEMS THERE'S BEEN AN ERROR.
THIS, AS YOU MAY HAVE GATHERED, WAS AN UNDERSTATEMENT.

IN THE WEEKS IT TOOK THEM TO REACH EARTH, NOX AND HER CREW LEARNED A GREAT MANY THINGS.
THEY'VE FENDED OFF FOUR ATTACKS.
SO IT'S TRUE. THE POWERS DID MANIFEST.
BUT...HOW?! WHERE'S THEIR HEART? THEY CAN'T GET THEIR POWERS WITHOUT IT, CAN THEY?
NOX, DID YOU KNOW THIS WAS A POSSIBILITY?
WE'RE ENTERING THEIR ATMOSPHERE.
BRACE FOR IMPACT.
THWAM

DO YOU THINK THAT'S A "SUMMER CONSTRUCTION" SOUND OR A "SOMETHING'S ABOUT TO TRY AND KILL US" SOUND?
PO-TAY-TO, PO-TAH-TO.
CRASH
YEEP!
BILL, GET THE KIDS OUT OF HERE!
I'M NOT LEAVING YOU!
GO BACK THE WAY YOU CAME IN. TAKE THE VAN.
SANDY, YOU CAN'T BE SERIOUS! COME ON!
CAN WE WATCH YOU FIGHT AN ALIEN?!
GO!
THWUNK

CRUNCH

HOLY CREPES.

WHERE IS IT?

OH MY FRIG, NOT *THIS* AGAIN!

WHATEVER IT IS YOU THINK WE HAVE, OR STOLE, OR DON'T DESERVE, I DON'T CARE! SILAS, SHOW 'EM WHAT YOU DO!
WHAT?

HE...LOOK, HE USUALLY TRANSFORMS, BUT WHATEVER. WE'LL TAKE YOU OUT ANYWAY!
HOW...?

GET OFF OF OUR PLANET!

OH MY STARS.
IT'S YOU.
NOX, WHAT?!

I WAS WRONG. I'VE BEEN WRONG THIS WHOLE TIME. IT'S NOT AN OBJECT, IT'S A PERSON.

YOU'RE THE HEART.
WHAT?

THIS ISN'T POSSIBLE.
A CONDUIT. SHE ENHANCES THEIR POWER...MAKES THEM STRONGER...

WAIT, HOW DO YOU KNOW THAT?
IS THAT WHAT'S HAPPENING?

THE STRENGTH.
WATCH IT!

THE SPIRIT.

...AND THE SIGHT.
NO WAY. ARE YOU SERIOUS?
THE FISH?
LIKE I SAID...

THEIR MATH WAS A LITTLE OFF.
NO WAY!

DO YOU HAVE ANY IDEA THE POWER CONTAINED WITHIN THIS CREATURE?
I... SOMETIMES HE TURNS INTO A TINY WHALE.
WITH LASERS. THAT PART'S IMPORTANT.

INFINITE KNOWLEDGE. THE SIGHT IS... WHOEVER POSSESSES IT IS THE KEY TO ALL THINGS, TO THESE ABILITIES. HE CAN TELL US EVERYTHING! DON'T YOU SEE? HE HAS ALL THE ANSWERS!
BUT...HE'S A GOLDFISH.

WAIT, HE CAN'T EVEN TALK?
NOPE.
DOES HE COMMUNICATE WITH HIS MIND?
DON'T THINK SO.

WELL.

WE'VE GOT OUR WORK CUT OUT FOR US.

CHAPTER SIX

SO LET ME GET THIS STRAIGHT:
SILAS...
MY GOLDFISH...
...IS THE ONLY ONE WHO KNOWS WHAT'S GOING ON?!
PRETTY MUCH, YEAH.

HUH. WELL, I GUESS WE'RE POOCHED, THEN. HE DOESN'T TALK MUCH.
IT'S TRUE THAT THE CREATURE'S LANGUAGE IS EXTREMELY LIMITED, BUT THAT DOESN'T MEAN WE'RE OUT OF OPTIONS.

YOU GETTING A READ OFF HIM?
FAINTLY. I CAN TELL HE WISHES TO EXPRESS HIMSELF, BUT IS UNABLE TO.

HOLD ON, YOU CAN TALK TO FISH?
MY FAMILY HAS A GIFT FOR COMMUNICATION AND EMPATHY. WE DEVELOPED THE TRANSLATORS THAT ALLOW US TO SPEAK WITH YOU NOW.

OH, THAT'S SUPER COOL! I WONDERED ABOUT THAT!
NEAT, ISN'T IT?

OTHER SPECIES HAVE ADAPTED IT, SUCH AS THE GRYPHON YOU BATTLED, WHICH IS UNFORTUNATE.
SHE WAS THE WORST! WE WHUPPED HER GOOD, THOUGH.

SHE HAS MANY SUPPORTERS WHO WILL SEE HER DEMISE AS A CHANCE TO USURP HER TITLE.

ANYBODY EVER TELL YOU YOUR VOICE IS REALLY SOOTHING?
FREQUENTLY, BUT I ENJOY IT.

AS FOR THE MATTER AT HAND, NO, I CANNOT "TALK TO FISH," BUT I FEEL THAT GIVEN SOME TIME, I MAY BE ABLE TO ESTABLISH A CONNECTION WITH HIM. WE MAY YET GET SOME ANSWERS.
ASK HIM IF HE LIKES THE SHRIMP FLAKES I GOT HIM!

SHAKA SHAKE

I MUST ASK YOU BOTH, BEFORE WE GO ANY FURTHER...HOW HAVE YOU MANAGED TO DEFEAT SO MANY ATTACKERS?

WE JUST SORT OF...FOUGHT THEM?
PLUS, AMIE'S GOT THAT THING WHERE SHE TOUCHES YOU AND YOU GET MORE POWERFUL.
KEVIN AND SANDY ARE PRETTY STRONG, AND SILAS BLASTED A COUPLE.
I DON'T REALLY GET HOW IT WORKS, BUT IT'S COOL.

FASCINATING. YOU DID IT ALL ON YOUR OWN, EVEN WITHOUT THE SIGHT'S KNOWLEDGE?
WELL, YEAH. WE KIND OF HAD TO.
BUT HOW COULD YOU--
NOX, BACK UP A STEP.

WE HAVE NOT INTRODUCED OURSELVES. I AM PRUE, AND THIS IS MY WIFE UNA. OUR COMPANION ROWAN, AND YOU'VE MET NOX. SHE IS OUR GUARDIAN.

WELL, YOU KNOW SILAS, SO I'M AMIE. THIS IS KEVIN. OUR FRIEND SANDY'S OUTSIDE, I THINK?
WHAT'S SHE UP TO?

CECILY, PICK UP! YOUR FATHER'S PHONE WON'T GO TO VOICEMAIL. **WHERE ARE YOU?**
SANDY?

WHAT'S WRONG?
MY FAMILY. I CAN'T GET AHOLD OF THEM SINCE I SENT THEM OFF AND THE CAR'S GONE.

EVERYTHING OKAY?
NO, EVERYTHING IS **NOT OKAY!**

ALIENS AND MONSTERS ARE FINE, BUT BILL AND THE KIDS? WHAT IF THEY'RE HURT?
WE'LL FIGURE THIS OUT, OKAY? WOULD THEY HAVE GONE HOME?
I CALLED THERE! **NOTHING!**

THEY COULD BE IN TRAFFIC.
CECILY IS ALWAYS ON HER PHONE. SHE WOULDN'T DO THIS.

SCREEEEE!

RREE!
RRRR!

CAR!
MOM!
CECILY! WHAT HAPPENED?!

THIS GIANT...THIS GIANT SNAKE, WE GOT HOME AND IT WAS WAITING, IT JUST GRABBED HIM AND--
YOUR FATHER? WHERE IS HE?

BEHIND US! IT'S COMING, IT HAS HIM, IT SAID YOUR NAMES AND--THIS ISN'T RAD ANYMORE, MOM! I'M SCARED!
HEY, HEY, KIDDO, IT'S OKAY. NOBODY'S GOING TO HURT YOUR DAD.

WELL NOW, I WOULDN'T SSSAY THAT.
GASP
GO, GET INSIDE!

IS THIS ONE OF YOURS?
NOPE. DEFINITELY EVIL.
NOX, DID YOU BRING YOUR LITTLE PLAYTHINGS ALL THIS WAY JUSSST TO SAY HELLO?
BACK OFF, WHATEVER YOU ARE!
YEAH!
IT DOESN'T MAKE SSSENSE. WHY WOULD GODLIKE POWERS GO TO PUNY ANIMALS LIKE YOU? AT LEASSST *THEY* LOOK THE PART.
WHAAA!
WHERE IS HE? WHERE'S BILL?
YOUR PRECIOUSSS HUSBAND? HE'S WITH THE OTHERS.
WHO DO YOU WORK FOR?
HA! YOU THINK I'M SSSOME LOW-LEVEL PAWN? YOU KILLED THE GRYPHON. I WAS HER AIDE FOR FOUR HUNDRED YEARS. I TOOK HER PLACE, GAINED HER STRENGTH, AND SOON I'LL HAVE YOURS AS WELL.
WHAM
COUNT YOURSELF LUCKY THAT YOU HAVE NO GIFTS, NOX. YOU'LL DIE QUICKER.
HEY, EARTHWORM!

KRA-POW!!
AUGH!
PRUE!
WOULD IT MAKE YOU FEEL BETTER IF I SAID "OW"?
NOD
AH!
CRACK
WOOO! NOW THAT, THAT HURT. A LITTLE BIT. KIND OF.

WHY ISN'T IT WORKING?!
HIS SKIN, IT'S LIKE...KICKING A VAULT DOOR.
HE'S TOO STRONG.
AW, SUSHI? YOU SHOULDN'T HAVE.
AMIE, CATCH!
THWAP!
AGH!
YOU ASKED FOR IT, CREEP.
SHOOOM!

COFF
COOF
HACK

HAAAHAHAHA! *YEAH!* THAT'S WHAT I'M TALKING ABOUT! YOU ACTUALLY DID SSSOME DAMAGE, KID!

PUTZ.

ARE YOU ALRIGHT?
I...I DO NOT KNOW. COMBAT IS NOT MY STRENGTH.

GO HELP YOUR FRIENDS. I'LL WATCH ROWAN AND MAKE SURE THEY'RE SAFE.
OKAY. I'LL BE BACK.

I LIKE HIS... ARMOR.

HOW'S THIS FOR DAMAGE?
WHAM

N-NOT BAD, ACTUALLY.

WHERE ARE OUR FRIENDS?!
I TOLD YOU, THEY'RE GONE. YOU DON'T NEED TO WORRY ABOUT THEM NOW.
LIAR!

I SEE YOUR PAIN, STRENGTH, BUT THE OTHERS...? THEY WERE NOTHING. NOT YOUR LOVERS OR FAMILIES, JUST THINGS HOLDING YOU BACK.

I FOLLOWED THE TRAILSSS, THE ENERGY FROM YOUR BATTLES. I FOUND THE WOMAN AT THE PET SHOP, THAT PATHETIC COUPLE... BUT THEY TOLD ME NOTHING. *NOTHING!*

TURNSSS OUT, ALL I HAD TO DO WAS WAIT FOR THOSE AWFUL CHILDREN TO LEAD ME RIGHT TO YOU.

KEVIN, PUT YOUR HAND ON AMIE'S.
HUH?
DO IT. NOW.
OH.

HAH HAH
AMIE? AMIE!

WAKE UP! COME ON, YOU HAVE TO WAKE UP!

WHA...
HUH?
WHERE AM I?

SANDY!

HUH?
NOPE, NUH UH, NOT AGAIN. I'M OUT.

SANDY, BABY! SWEETHEART, WAKE UP! WHO DID THIS?!
THEY COMBINED THEIR POWERS SOMEHOW, ALL OF THEM...I THINK IT WAS TOO MUCH.
NO, NO! THIS ISN'T HAPPENING!

SANDY, PLEASE! I NEED YOU!

H...HEY...
AMIE!
IT'S...OKAY... R-REMEMBER?
HEALING POWERS.
B...BILL?
SANDY!

HEY THERE, BIG GUY. TAKE IT EASY.
YOU'RE OKAY.
UNGH...

THAT... HURT.
YOU SAVED US AGAIN. QUITE THE TRACK RECORD, MVP.

OW!

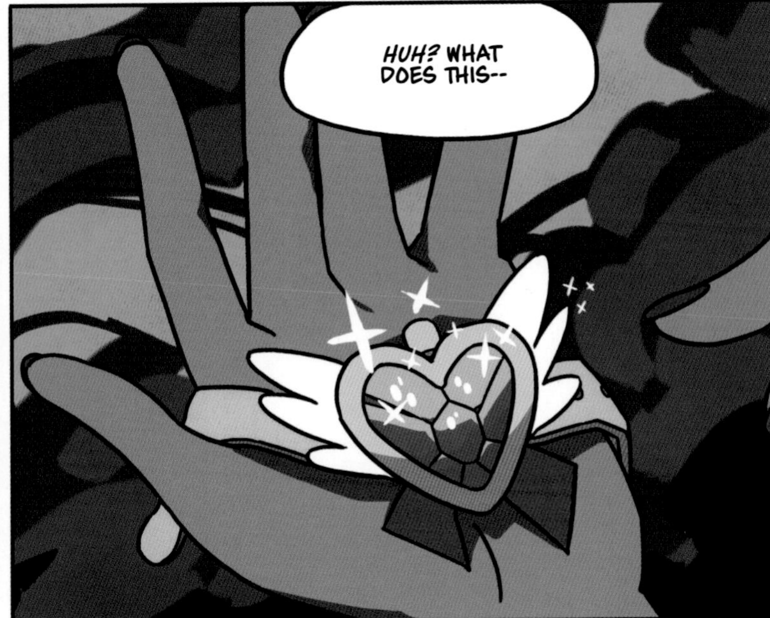
HUH? WHAT DOES THIS--

KLIK

KLIK

HUH.

...IT'S NOT WORKING.
THE HEALING MUST ONLY WORK ON YOU FOUR.

HOW ARE THEY?
ROWAN? CAN YOU HEAR US?
THEY'RE HURT, BUT THEY WILL BE ALRIGHT.

I CAN'T FIX THIS.
GIVE IT TIME, AMIE. ROWAN'S FAMILY IS VERY STRONG.
I WISH THIS MADE SENSE. I WANT TO HELP EVERYONE, NOT JUST US.

YOU HAVE HELPED SO MANY ALREADY. LOOK AT WHAT YOU CAN DO. YOUR FRIENDS ARE POWERFUL, BUT YOU MAKE THEM INTO SOMETHING ELSE ENTIRELY.

YOU MAY NOT REALIZE IT, BUT YOUR GIFTS ARE THE STRONGEST OF ALL.
"SHE'S RIGHT, YOU KNOW."

ONE MONTH LATER...
"AMIE IS EXTRAORDINARY."

HAH!
BLOOP

VERY GOOD! NOW, LET'S SEE IF WE CAN'T GET HIM TO USE THOSE LASERS!
"SHE'LL GET THERE, ESPECIALLY WITH ALL THIS TRAINING."
"NOX IS QUITE DEDICATED."

SHE'S PRETTY INTENSE. HAD ME RUNNING LAPS LAST WEEK, NEARLY COUGHED UP A LUNG.
CAN HUMANS DO THAT?
OH YEAH, IT'S PRETTY COMMON.

DISGUSTING.

HEY KEV, YOU WANT TO PRACTICE TANDEM BLASTS? I THINK I KNOW HOW TO AIM, FINALLY!

DUTY CALLS.

THAT'S WHAT YOU SAID LAST TIME!

FWEET
IN THE END, THINGS SORT OF WORKED OUT.

NOX STAYED ON TO TRAIN US, HAVING FINALLY FOUND HER PURPOSE.

THE BAD GUYS DIDN'T STOP COMING, BUT WE LEARNED TO BE PREPARED.

WE STARTED TO UNDERSTAND WHAT WE WERE CAPABLE OF.
SPORT

GRAND OPENING
SALE!
CUT
IT WASN'T NORMAL, NOT REALLY, BUT IT WAS GOOD-- THE BEST IT HAD BEEN SINCE THE LIGHT FIRST HIT.

TWO OF THE WARRIORS LEFT, FINALLY ABLE TO HAVE A PEACEFUL LIFE TOGETHER.

THE OTHER MOVED IN.
BOOK. THIS IS A BOOK. CAN YOU SAY "BOOK"?

THIS LITTLE FISHY NEEDS SOME FOOD! I'LL DROP HIM BY AGAIN NEXT WEEK, I PROMISE!
I'M GETTING CLOSE, I KNOW IT!

C'MON, TEACH. LET'S GET SOME GRUB.
CAN WE ORDER THOSE..."GARLIC FINGERS"?

THERE YOU GO, SILAS. HOME SWEET HOME.
THERE ARE WORLDS OF KNOWLEDGE I WISH I COULD SHARE WITH THEM.

C'MON, ARDMORE! GOT YOU SOME SNAILS FOR DINNER, YUM!
ANSWERS TO THE GREAT QUESTIONS, THE KEYS TO THEIR ABILITIES...

HOW'S THAT FOR GOURMET, LITTLE GUY? FRESH AND TASTY!
WHAT'S COMING, AND HOW TO STOP IT.

I DON'T CARE IF YOU CAN'T TALK, FISH-A-WISH. YOU'RE THE BEST MAGIC COMPANION A GIRL COULD ASK FOR.
STILL, WITHOUT MY HELP, THEY MANAGED TO FIGURE OUT THE MOST IMPORTANT THING:

BE BACK IN A FLASH, CUTIES! YOU'RE IN CHARGE!
WE'RE MORE POWERFUL TOGETHER.

KLIK
THE END

HOW TO DRAW OUR HEROES!

COVER GALLERY

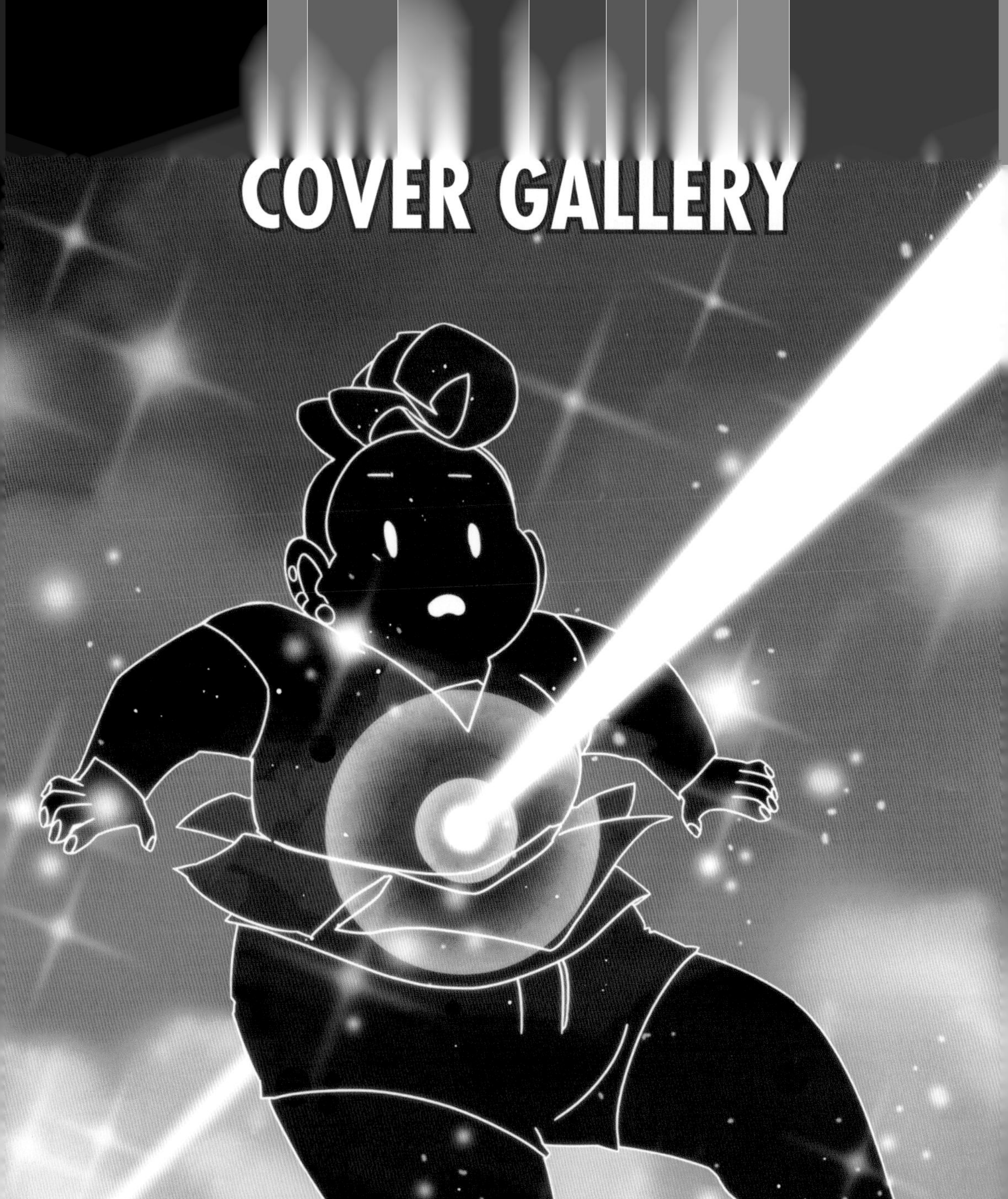

ISSUE ONE COVER BY
MATT CUMMINGS

ISSUE ONE BOOM! TEN YEARS EXCLUSIVE COVER BY
LUCY KNISLEY

10

ISSUE ONE VARIANT COVER BY
BABS TARR

ISSUE ONE UNLOCKED RETAILER VARIANT COVER BY
IAN McGINTY
WITH COLORS BY RIAN SYGH

ISSUE ONE THIRD EYE COMICS EXCLUSIVE COVER BY
STEPHANIE GONZAGA

ISSUE TWO COVER BY
MATT CUMMINGS

ISSUE THREE COVER BY
MATT CUMMINGS

ISSUE FOUR COVER BY
MATT CUMMINGS

ISSUE FIVE COVER BY
MATT CUMMINGS

ISSUE SIX COVER BY
MATT CUMMINGS